About a week befor *a ringing phone.*

"You might want to sit down, Mr. Romero." Somehow the smile transmitted over telephone wires. Excitement built in Steve's heart and tingled to his fingertips, where the earphone trembled in his hand. He stood, frozen in place, waiting for the announcement.

"Do you have a current passport?"

Passport? Romania! Sweat poured down his arms, and the phone slipped in his hand.

"Ah, yes, does this mean—"

"Congratulations! Your application has been approved! How soon can you fly to Bucharest?"

"You will like the director," Anika told Steve as they headed for the orphanage. "She is a sweet saint of God."

"But all is not sweetness in the children's home," Radu interjected. "I hear the American news has reported on our orphans." The statement ended like a question.

Steve nodded his assent. "The situation sounded grim." He didn't elaborate.

"The situation is sad. But God is at work." A peaceful smile lit Radu's face. "He has used those reports to bring many foreigners to our country to adopt the children. Good from evil. Like your own tragedy." He never minced words.

The string of words couldn't penetrate Steve's excitement. "I can't wait. Ever since the idea of adoption occurred to me, I've been hungry for a child to call my own. After what happened here—" Momentarily his voice faltered. "Romania was one of the first places I thought of."

"And this afternoon you may find your answer. Here we are."

DARLENE FRANKLIN lives in Denver at the foot of the Rocky Mountains with her mother and her cat, Puff. A few years ago, suddenly a single mother of two children, she discovered the greatest romance of all—the God who loves "no matter what." That love, plus a lifelong interest in missions, fuels her writing. She likes to read, create cross-stitch patterns, teach Sunday school, and scrapbook.

Romanian Rhapsody

Darlene Franklin

Heartsong Presents

A note from the Author:
I love to hear from my readers! You may correspond with me by writing:

Darlene Franklin
Author Relations
PO Box 719
Uhrichsville, OH 44683

ISBN 1-59310-549-5

ROMANIAN RHAPSODY

Our mission is to publish and distribute inspirational products offering exceptional value and biblical encouragement to the masses.

All Scripture quotations are taken from the King James Version of the Bible.

All of the characters and events in this book are fictitious. Any resemblance to actual persons, living or dead, or to actual events is purely coincidental.

PRINTED IN THE U.S.A.

one

"Rule number one: Pack light," Carrie recited, running fingers through her short brown hair. Despite her best efforts, her performance gowns, three pairs of jeans, five T-shirts (two of them emblazoned Victory Singers—Romania Tour), underwear, music, camera, and Bible barely fit into the one suitcase and one carry-on she was allowed on the plane.

Carrie glanced at the clock. 2:00 p.m. Time to kill until the first meeting and rehearsal at five o'clock. *When will my roommate get here?* She looked at the empty bed. Maybe from a part of the country as foreign to her as—Romania! She laughed at herself, the sound laced with excitement. *This is the beginning—the beginning of the adventure.*

A key turned in the door, and a maid wearing a loose-fitting maternity dress appeared in the doorway. But where was her cleaning cart?

The woman waited by the door, carrying on a conversation with someone hidden from view.

"You need to rest after that trip," a man spoke.

"Don't worry." Arms lifted as if in an embrace, the rustling of two bodies entwining, and then the woman entered the room, pulling two bags with her. Dark-haired, tall, and slender, she was heavily pregnant. She turned to Carrie with a wide smile.

"Hi! You must be my roommate." She plunked her bags down on the empty bed.

Carrie tried not to stare. She had expected a roomie like her best friend, Joan, another college junior, perhaps—not a mother-to-be. She found her voice. "Yes. Carrie Randolph from Penn State. Soprano."

"And I'm Lila Romero. Alto. Steve and I planned on one more trip with the Victory Singers after I graduated from CU last year. I never thought I'd be as big as a house by this summer!" She patted her belly and giggled. "God decided to bless us earlier than we planned." She reached out to shake Carrie's hand.

The *C* states paraded through Carrie's mind—Connecticut, Carolina, California. "Colorado?" she confirmed as Lila's hand gripped hers, long fingers squeezing into her palm.

"Uh-huh." Lila rummaged through her suitcase, arranging her belongings in the bureau.

"When is the baby due?" By her size, she looked like she would deliver while they were in Romania.

"In about ten weeks. I may go into labor on Labor Day." She laughed, a light sound that tinkled like a glockenspiel.

"I'm surprised you and—Steve? That's your husband?—aren't staying together." Carrie sat down on her bed and watched Lila unpack.

"Oh. Well. We're used to it, touring this way. It's our first trip with the Singers since our marriage. I think it's a lark. I get to pretend I'm just one of the girls again." She flashed a smile at Carrie. "I'm looking forward to it."

Some of Carrie's uneasiness lifted, and she found herself smiling back. "Yeah, it will be fun."

Lila slipped out of her dress and shrugged on a voluminous robe. "And Steve and I are planning on a second honeymoon after the tour, in Constanta on the Black Sea. Gloriously romantic." She stiffened for a second and then relaxed.

"Something the matter?"

"Just Braxton Hicks contractions."

Contractions?

She hastened to add, "Practice contractions. To make the

actual labor easier, if that's possible." She yawned. "Steve was right. I am tired." Taking a tiny travel alarm, one of those the size of a mouse but that probably had a growl like an angry cat, she set the time. "If you don't mind, I'll rest for a little bit." She ducked under the sheets before Carrie could respond.

Carrie took out her music, turned on the pole lamp between two chairs, and started humming through her parts. One song called for a soprano solo. Maybe the director, Tim North, would ask her to sing it. She tried to shake away the thought. With thirty of the best singers from around the country, he could choose from plenty of talent. She practiced the solo anyway, then went back and hummed through the regular part.

The alarm sounded, as loud as an ambulance siren, and Carrie woke up, music still clutched to her chest. Lila sat on the floor, dressed in a loose-fitting sweat suit, doing some kind of stretching exercises. With an awkward push, she heaved herself up from the floor. "There's just about time to take a shower. Do you mind?"

Carrie shook her head, and soon water splashed in the bathroom like a distant waterfall. In her packet she found the blue-and-white name tag that read, "Hello! My name is. . . ," in English and Romanian. She slapped it on her Victory Singers shirt. Moths fluttered in her stomach. She didn't know anyone. She had met Tim only once, at the audition, and now Lila.

Someone knocked on the door. A young man, past college age, with crisp dark curls that sprang up on his head like grass after a rain, leaned on the doorpost. Pretty is as pretty does, but he certainly was handsome.

"Hi! You must be Steve. Lila's just taking a shower." She waved him inside.

"And you are"—he peered at her name tag—"Carrie Randolph. *Incantat de cunostinta*—I'm glad to meet you, Carrie." He sat down on Lila's bed.

"Do you speak Romanian?" Carrie asked, fascinated.

"Just phrases from a Berlitz book that I've practiced."

Lila came out, already dressed, toweling her hair dry. "Hi, sweetheart." She kissed the top of Steve's head and rummaged through the nightstand drawer for a brush. "You've already met Carrie?"

Carrie ducked into the bathroom, brushed her teeth, and checked her watch. Quarter to five—was it too early to go downstairs? No.

Picking up her purse, she headed for the door. "See you folks later, then."

"In just a minute." With a few strokes, Lila had restored her hair to a lovely free-falling style.

About a dozen people wearing identical blue-and-white name tags congregated by the elevator. Even without the tags, the undercurrent of voices humming and feet tapping in time to piped-in music gave them away as musicians. *Maybe the name tags aren't so silly.* They had only three days to move from strangers to a cohesive choir.

The group steered toward a smallish room, the Franklin. Someone dropped a rehearsal folder, and the sound reverberated around the walls. A magnificent grand piano dominated one corner. *Where's Tim? There he is.*

At the opposite end of the room, a man with long graying hair who looked like he might have been a hippie back in the '60s directed the new arrivals. "Sopranos, altos, tenors, bass—left to right. Musicians, your instrument cases are by the piano." To Carrie's surprise, Steve moved toward the keyboard, pulled out the bench, and plunked out a few chords. The sweet harmonics carried into the air.

Carrie found a seat on the front row, where the short people would sit. *If for once I could stand on the back row!* A petite blonde with long, curving hair that Carrie envied took a place next to her.

"Hi! I'm Amy Knight. Is this your first year? It's mine and. . ." The girl continued speaking, clearly as nervous as Carrie felt. She relaxed and started the process of introducing herself.

❧

Steve flexed his fingers and ran through some arpeggios while he scanned the new group. A few familiar faces returned from last year, but he and Tim were the only people left from the original Victory Singers who went to Ireland five years ago. Lila had joined the next tour, after her freshman year at CU.

He glanced where his wife waited, leaning over the chair and chatting with one of last year's returnees. He smiled. Marrying Lila was the best thing that ever happened to him, that and the baby. He squashed a frown that tried to cross his lips. The doctor said he shouldn't worry; travel was fine until the last month.

"Hey, Steve, give me a C!" the trumpeter called. Trust Guy, another old-timer from the second year forward, to keep them on track.

"Sure." He pounded down on middle C five times while around him instrumentalists tuned up, creating the dreadful cacophony that preceded a musical event.

His eyes wandered to the right, and he picked out Lila's roommate in the soprano section. She reminded him a lot of Lila that first year—the same short brown hair, the way she perched on the edge of her seat, engaged in animated conversation with the girl next to her. Her finger jabbed at the paper in her hands, first a smile, then a frown crossing her face. What caused the consternation? He glanced at his own schedule to check. Bold print announced that Carrie Randolph would back up Amy Knight's solo. His eyebrows rose. She must be good to beat out other talented, experienced singers. No need for her to frown.

"Hey, Uncle Steve, can I play?" A five-year-old body wiggled next to him on the piano bench.

"Just for a minute. Your Dad's about to get started." He scooted over so his nephew, the son of his sister Brenda and director Tim, could reach the keyboard more easily.

Maybe Lila and I will have a little boy like this, he mused, stopping his hands from rubbing the child's head so he wouldn't break his concentration. *A boy with dark curly hair and brilliant black eyes who loves music.*

A loud squawk interrupted his thoughts. "Testing, testing." Someone adjusted the volume, and Tim's voice rang out clear. "Welcome to the Victory Singers Romania Tour."

After five years, Steve could have given the speech himself. Get to rehearsals on time. When we get overseas, be careful what you drink. Sodas and bottled or boiled water are best; never ever drink from the tap. Instead of Montezuma, you'll have Ceausescu after you. At that, the group laughed like a programmed sound track. You'll be traveling as an American in a foreign country. You represent Jesus Christ, and the good old USA. Learn those Romanian phrases, and above all practice the art of patience.

Tim stopped speaking, and low-level noise rose as chairs pushed back and papers inside music folders rustled. Steve nervously played through a few bars of "Victory in Jesus," the group's theme song. The newest version of Victory Singers was under way.

❧

A local news anchor said good night when Lila entered the hotel room later that night. Carrie looked up from the desk where she was finishing a letter.

"Hi there! Where have you been?" *Silly question. With her husband, of course.*

"Seeing Steve's sister off at the airport. Little Sammy wouldn't say good-bye to Tim and turned his head away. It would have been funny if it wasn't so sad."

Tim? As in Tim North, the director?

Lila sat down on the edge of the bed, kicked off her shoes, and wiggled her toes with relief. "That feels good. You know, I should go to sleep. Long day tomorrow and all that."

"Me, too." They let out simultaneous long, dramatic sighs and grinned at each other. "I'm too excited," Carrie admitted. She signed the letter and stuck it in an envelope, then tucked pen and paper back into the luggage. She grabbed her camera.

"I'm not sleepy either, even though this is my fourth trip." Lila unearthed a ball of pastel ombré yarn and began crocheting a chain. "—thirteen, fourteen, fifteen. That should do it."

"What are you making?" Carrie asked, snapping a picture while Lila continued working.

"Oh, a sweater for the baby. The blanket was too bulky to carry on the plane, but I figured I could squeeze in a ball of yarn and a crochet hook. This will be a sleeve." The chain dangled in front of her. "Some day."

"My grandmother tried to teach me. But I wasn't interested, not enough to really learn."

"Me either. At least, not until the baby."

"Have you picked out any names?"

"Nothing definite." Lila shook her head, an expression of amusement mixed with exasperation crossing her face. "I want to use the name Steven somewhere in a boy's name—the ultrasound shows it's probably a boy, although we don't know for sure—but he says no way, one Steve is enough." She leaned back. The chain was now a couple of rows deep. "A girl's name was easy. Brandi Lynn, just because we like the sound of it. Steve is lobbying for Brandon for a boy's name. Keep it simple, he says."

Lila looked so maternal sitting there, crochet hook slipping through the yarn. Carrie felt a twinge of envy for the family

Lila already had—Steve, Tim, his wife, young Sammy.

"I just love children!" The words blurted out. Hands still working, Lila glanced up as if waiting for Carrie to continue.

Encouraged, she went on. "I plan on working with children in some capacity. Maybe I'm trying to make up for being an only child."

"An only child?" Lila studied her roommate. "That must have been lonely. No brothers or sisters—"

"And now that I'm grown up, no nieces or nephews either. I'll have to marry someone with a large family, so I can claim his."

Somewhere nearby a clock bell tolled. "Midnight!" Lila rolled up the sleeve, now a couple of inches long. "Time for Cinderella to go to bed. Lights out?"

"In a minute." After the final evening toiletries, Carrie slipped into the bed. She turned out the lamp and whispered into the darkened room. "Tonight, New York. This week, the world! Bucharest, anyway."

❧

A few days later, on the plane, Carrie punched the pillow with her fist, leaned back, and shut her eyes. Who could sleep, with the never-ending panorama unfolding right outside the window? East, east the plane flew.

Someone passed down the aisle on the way to the rest room. She peeked at her watch. 3:00 p.m. in Bucharest. Early morning back home. They should arrive at their destination in three hours. She straightened her chair with a snap and stuffed the pillow overhead. Day blended into sleepless night, but she didn't want to miss a minute of the adventure.

Bucharest was only the first stop. They would sweep through the southeastern portion of Romania, angle through the Carpathian Mountains, follow the Danube River, which formed the border with Bulgaria, and end in Constanta on the Black Sea. She hummed a few bars of "The Beautiful Blue Danube" and tapped her cramped feet to the waltz rhythm.

Romania. She still couldn't believe it. Land of the Romans. Transylvania, birthplace of the vampire legends. Homeland of Nadia Comaneci. Victim of Nicolae Ceausescu's policies until Romania proclaimed its independence from Soviet domination.

A stewardess stopped by the seat. "Can I get you something?"

Carrie started to say no, then reconsidered. "Some orange juice."

She stretched out her legs and sighed. People packed in, nine across separated only by two thin aisles usually blocked by stewardesses or people headed for the bathrooms. After seven hours, she was uncomfortable, and her leg muscles cramped. She decided to take a walk and angled her legs over her sleeping seatmates. *Is anyone else awake?*

Two rows behind her Lila slept soundly, head nestled against Steve's shoulder as if he were an eiderdown pillow. He popped one eye open when she passed by. He nodded at her, smiling slightly. "Can't sleep, huh?"

She shook her head. "Too excited, I guess."

"Me, too. Even after all these years." He pressed his nose against the window. "Look at that sky! Some day I want to write a rhapsody to celebrate the vistas I've seen from airplanes around the world."

"Are you a composer then?" Carrie questioned, interested.

"Nah. Just a wannabe, a high school music teacher with dreams beyond his reach." Disappointment flitted across his face.

"I don't know about that. Working with teenagers—that's tough. If you can help them grow up, you should feel good about what you are doing." *That's me, all right. Trying to solve everyone else's problems.*

"Yeah." An awed smile crossed his face, and he shifted his embrace of Lila. "The baby just kicked. I want to help this kid, at least, grow up well."

"That's beautiful." Carrie sucked the last of her juice, and a wave of tiredness washed over her. "Maybe I am sleepy after all. I'll try to catch some shut-eye. See you in Romania!"

A few hours later, they landed in Bucharest. "This way, please." In a lightly accented voice, a pert young brunette directed Carrie to where the others were waiting. Momentarily isolated among people speaking a Babel of languages, not one of them English, she felt a moment's hesitation. Noticing the numerous flags in Romania's colors of red, yellow, and black, reality hit home. *I'm really in Romania!* She hurried to rejoin the group.

Tim checked his list. "Everyone's here. Our bus should be ready, so let's head for the exit."

Carrie's heart sank when she saw the bus, their home away from home for the next two weeks. It most resembled a yellow school bus, as old as the ones from her childhood and probably less comfortable to adult dimensions. She glanced at Lila. How would she manage?

Within minutes the bus was jolting down city streets. Eager to see as much as possible before the sun went down, Carrie cleaned off the window.

"It's all so new! I expected older buildings. After all, Romania has been around since Roman times."

Steve overheard her. "Another crime to lay at Ceausescu's door. He wasn't much into historic preservation—wanted to build a monument to himself instead."

"Look, there it is!" Lila pointed. "The Palace of the People on Victory of Socialism Boulevard. What a silly name." She paused. "But lovely, nonetheless." Her face tightened in pain. "Maybe a pillow will soften the bumps."

Soon they arrived at the hotel, and Tim gave room assignments.

"We're all on the second floor," Steve announced. He

hoisted Lila's bag in his hand. "Of course there's no elevator." His mouth twitched in a grin. Accepting his arm for support, Lila had to stop midway to catch her breath.

A foot into the room, Carrie halted abruptly. A dingy washbasin stood in one corner, and a single bed dominated the tiny space.

Steve moved past her and dropped the suitcases in the corner. "Need anything else tonight?"

"No, I don't think so." Lila kissed him good night. "See you in the morning."

The two women were left alone in the room. "I was afraid of this," Lila admitted to Carrie. "We'll have to share a bed. I'll try not to snuggle up next to you!" Her laugh sounded forced.

❧

Carrie was swimming through a gulf-warm pool, almost drowning in the water.

"Wake up, Carrie, you've got to help me."

Lila's near-hysterical voice pierced through the fog of Carrie's dream. She sat up. *It wasn't a dream.* The bed was sopping wet, warm, and sticky. "What—?"

"I thought you'd never wake up." Lila's alto voice rose to coloratura soprano. "You've got to get Steve for me."

The panic on Lila's face registered with Carrie, and her mind collated the facts—Lila's pregnancy, the wet bed—*Labor?*

"My water's broken. Those weren't false labor pains earlier. It's the real thing."

Fighting panic, Carrie asked, "Which room?"

"201—last door on the right." Lila's face clenched in pain as a renewed contraction hit. "Hurry!"

Carrie pulled on a pair of jeans and a T-shirt and ran out into the hall.

two

Strong harsh knocks hammered the door. The knob rattled as someone tried to open it. Tim was already pulling on his jeans when Steve fought his way out of a deep sleep.

When he opened the door, still in a sleepy daze, for a second Steve thought he saw Lila outlined by the dim hotel light. Then his eyes focused, and he realized it was Carrie.

"Steve—Lila's in labor. You've got to come." She started back down the hall, then paused when he didn't immediately follow.

"Labor?" His sleep-drugged mind was trying to comprehend. "But that's impossible!"

"Her water's broken. Hurry!"

"I'll be there as soon as I throw some clothes on." *Oh, God, no! Help!*

"I'll get a taxi." Tim picked up the phone and dialed the operator. "No answer. The switchboard must be closed at night. I'll take care of it. You get Lila."

Steve nodded his head, not really hearing his words. *Lila.* Heart-pounding adrenaline speeded his every move, and he ran out the door and down the hall in less than a minute.

Carrie flung open the door at his first tap. The bed with its sopping wet sheets testified to Carrie's story. Where was Lila?

"Where is she?"

"Right here." Lila squatted in a chair, her suitcase on the floor in front of her. Carrie rummaged through the nightstand and pulled out deodorant, a hair brush, and a change of clothes.

By their front door in Denver, an overnight bag waited,

packed in readiness for this moment since the fifth month. *It's not supposed to be like this! The baby's not supposed to be born until Labor Day!* Steve shoved the panicked thoughts aside.

"Everyone says this is the easy part." Tear-filled eyes looked to him for reassurance. "But the childbirth manual didn't come with instructions for premature labor. Uh oh, here comes another one." She clenched the sides of her chair. The material stretched across her abdomen crawled in an eerie imitation of a line dance as Steve watched, stunned.

She relaxed. "Eight minutes that time."

He hurried to her side and gripped her sweat-dampened hands between his. She smiled, as if she were trying to encourage him. "The baby will be all right."

He's got to be. "Of course. Babies are born early all the time." *Not this early.*

"But the doctor said I was fine for another month. I don't want my baby born in some foreign hospital!" Lila fought back tears. "I wonder if the hospital even has a neonatal unit." Her words echoed Steve's fears.

"We'll get you home as soon as possible," he promised. "Whatever it costs."

Their eyes locked, a mingled worry and excitement forging yet another link to the chain that bound them together.

The suitcase snapped shut. "That should do it," Carrie announced. "Where do we go?"

"You don't have to come." Steve wasn't sure if he wanted this girl—a total stranger less than a week ago—to encroach on this most intimate moment.

He could feel Carrie looking at them. "Well, take the bag with you," she said and handed the suitcase to Steve. When he grabbed it, her face crumpled like a used hankie, disappointment sketched on her mobile features.

"I would appreciate your company. Please come." Even in

her pain, Lila's kindness won out. Pride in his wife and shame at himself chastened Steve. "You can be the honorary aunt," Lila offered.

The wrinkles on Carrie's face reversed direction as she grinned widely. "I'd like that." Currents Steve didn't understand underlined her voice, as if some unspoken communication had passed between the two women.

Another contraction hit as Lila descended the stairs. She flattened her back against the wall and gripped the handrail. Steve glanced at his watch—eight, eight and a half minutes? The second hand on the dial swept around slowly.

In the lobby Tim paced. "I finally raised the concierge. He's called a taxi. I contacted Radu, the pastor here, too. He'll meet us at the hospital." He looked straight at Lila. "How are you doing?"

"Okay, so far. It's the baby I'm worried about." She teetered over to the only chair in the lobby, a straight-backed, uncomfortable fixture with torn upholstery. Ten minutes and another contraction later, the taxi arrived.

The cab driver made up in speed what his car lacked in springs, racing over bumps that bounced them around in the backseat like loose basketballs. At one extra large pothole, Lila cried out. Another contraction? Yes. Steve checked his watch. *Lord, please help us!* Seven minutes that time. *How far away is the hospital?*

The taxi's headlights shone on a small rectangular hospital sign. Not one overhead lamp illuminated the tiny parking lot, and only one dim yellow bulb announced the entrance. Tim thrust a handful of *lei* at the driver as they scrambled out of the car.

A short, heavyset man with thick gray hair and Slavic features hurried out to them from the doorway and waved them inside. "Brother Tim. Come." He took Lila by the hand and led her toward the front desk. "You must be Mrs. Romero. This way please. They expect you."

Steve hadn't expected the Latin accent, rhythms familiar from working with Hispanic students in band. *I'm glad we have someone—anyone!—to translate.* The suitcase swung from his hand as he trotted along behind.

He pulled up short when he shouldered through the revolving door. He had been to emergency rooms a few times with band students, and he had somehow expected the same bustling efficiency. Instead, two groups huddled in shadowy corners, talking in quiet whispers amid low sobbing. Pastor Radu motioned for him to join Lila at the receptionist desk. *Paperwork and red tape are universal constants.*

Another contraction began—six and a half minutes this time. Steve swallowed hard, trying to control his irritation and fear. "Can't you take my wife to the maternity ward? Give her something?"

Pastor Radu relayed the request to the receptionist. She shook her head firmly. He translated her reply.

"The doctor is not here yet, she says. It is a first baby. There is time yet. Be patient."

Sweat beaded on Lila's forehead. She tried to smile, but pain lines flattened out her lips. "The breathing exercises—like we practiced—" Her words dwindled to a whimper of pain.

"I'll answer the questions," Tim volunteered. "You take care of Lila."

"Look at me." Steve knelt next to his wife and cradled her hands in his own. "Breathe deep and relax. You remember how." When he mirrored her breathing—one deep breath, three short puffs—he felt his own muscles relaxing. A grin built from the inside out. Maybe everything would turn out all right.

"I can't believe this is happening." She rubbed her hands over her abdomen. "Hello in there. I'll be seeing you soon."

Her bright dark eyes stared into Steve's, calling his soul. "I'm sure the baby will be okay." The reassurance was meant for herself as much as for him, he guessed.

She turned to Pastor Radu. "They have contacted a pediatrician, haven't they?"

He exchanged more words with the nurse. "No pediatrician. Only the doctor on call."

"Wait a minute." *This is too much.* "The baby is premature. Ten weeks early. There—must—be—a—pediatrician on hand when he is born."

The expression on Radu's face registered his understanding of the emergency. He spoke again with the nurse and translated, his face concerned. "The staff pediatrician is out of the city for the weekend. There is no one to call."

Lila grabbed Steve's hand, panic written on her face, as if begging him to make the nightmare go away. It was pointless to try to control his own fear.

At that point, the nurse shuffled her papers into a pile, signaling the interview was over. She motioned for Lila to follow her. Steve fell in behind, but the nurse put up both hands in front of her chest in a gesture that clearly said stop.

"Fathers wait here," the pastor explained. "The doctor will see you soon." He pointed behind Steve. "She can come."

Carrie stirred. She squeezed his arm. "I'll do my best," she promised. She grabbed the suitcase and followed Lila.

Before the door slammed shut, Lila twisted her head for one final glance, her face filled with a mixture of fear, loneliness, hope, and excitement. When Steve tried to follow, the handle turned in a one-way lock.

❧

Carrie traipsed down the hallway after Lila and the nurse. Behind a glass wall she glimpsed a nursery, one nurse watching over a room full of bassinets that all looked occupied.

Staring back over her shoulder, she nearly ran into their escort, who was pointing to the one empty bed in a ward full of women.

The sheets looked dingy gray, as if they were washed too infrequently or were old. An awful smell hung in the air, a mixture of disinfectant and sour milk. A gagging lump formed in Carrie's throat, which she forced down. Somehow she had to be strong for Lila.

The nurse handed Lila a hospital gown and indicated that she should change. She pulled a ringed curtain partway around the bed and disappeared.

Lila waited out the next contraction. "Seven minutes. I hope the doctor gets here soon. I hope he speaks English." Tears glistened in her eyes. "It's not supposed to be like this. Haven't they heard of Lamaze here? I want Steve." She sucked in her breath and patted Carrie's hand. "I'm sorry. I'm being rude. I'm very glad you're here." Strings dangled from the back of the yellow hospital gown when she drew it up her arms. "Tie it for me, please?"

"Sure." Carrie's hands trembled as she fumbled with the knots. A moan escaped Lila's lips, and Carrie looked into the face contorted with pain. Again she fought down a rising feeling of panic. Her only experience with hospitals came from having a tonsillectomy when she was five.

Somewhere a radio played rock songs in Romanian. Close by, a woman alternately cried and giggled. Metal clanged. Bed pans, maybe? *I haven't seen a doctor since we got here.* She wished she were back at the hotel—anywhere but here, in a maternity ward in a foreign hospital where only she and Lila spoke the same language. *Why did I offer to help?*

Lila's hand touched her arm. *Because of her.* Between sweat and tears, Lila's face gleamed. Carrie grabbed a towel and peeked around the edge of the curtain. In a far corner she spied a sink. "Be right back." The water ran lukewarm. Carrie soaked the towel, wrung it out, and hurried back to Lila's side. Another contraction had started. Carrie looked at her watch—six minutes, as far as she could tell. *The doctor better arrive soon.*

She sponged Lila's face. "How can I help?"

"Just having you here helps." Lila tried to smile but failed. "Do you happen to know Lamaze? Silly question. I'm supposed to relax and regain strength between contractions. Only they're much worse than I was prepared for. One ends, and I wonder how I can survive the next one—and the one after that—hours on end." Fat tears rolled down her face. "I suppose I sound like a crybaby."

"No." Carrie spoke softly. "I think you're incredibly brave." She sponged Lila's face again.

"At least we have the nursery all set up. Back home. Steve was so cute, ordering the crib as soon as the doctor confirmed my pregnancy. We even picked out the outfit to bring the baby home in." This time her smile held a little more real warmth. "I should look on the bright side. I get to shave two months off my pregnancy." She addressed her abdomen. "I don't care what you have to wear. I just want you to be healthy." She started to cry.

"I'm sure the baby will be fine." *I'm lying.* Carrie perched on the edge of the bed. *Change the subject.* "I hope someday I find someone as special as Steve. Handsome, talented, loves kids—" She broke off, a blush staining her cheeks with heat.

"You will." Lila spoke with calm assurance, pain free for the moment. "When God brings you together."

The calm shattered. "Aaah!" Lila's body jerked flat as another contraction hit. She grabbed Carrie's hand and squeezed hard enough to leave bruises, then let go. Seconds ticked by. Lila's abdomen stopped heaving with contractions. Lila remained motionless on the bed.

Watching Lila go through labor was enough to frighten a woman from ever having a baby. Carrie quieted her doubts. *She needs my reassurance, not an echo of her own fear.* Ready to pray, to listen, to do whatever she could to help, Carrie bent over the prostrate form, looking at the eyelids closed as if in sleep. *Something's wrong.* She felt Lila's wrist—no pulse! Wrong, a faint pulse throbbed deep down.

"Lila?" *Please wake up.*

"Lila?" Carrie spoke louder this time, loud enough to wake all the women on the ward. Lila didn't answer.

"Lila?" This time it came out a whisper. *Something's terribly wrong.* Panic built into a terrified scream as Carrie jerked back the curtain and yelled for help.

❧

When Steve heard Carrie scream, he jumped up and rammed the door, pounding with his fists as if the glass would break. The nurse stormed toward him, finger shaking with unmistakable authority. Then she, too, paused, listening to the sounds issuing from the ward.

Carrie's face pasted against the door, and Steve almost fell through the door when she succeeded in opening it. "Where's the doctor?" Her panicked voice echoed the fear in Steve's heart.

"Here I am." A voice spoke in British-toned English. Behind them appeared a young man. *He's no older than I am. Is he the doctor?* "Where is the patient?"

"In here." Carrie held the door open for Steve to squeeze through inches behind the doctor.

"How far apart are the contractions?"

"I don't know. Six minutes the last time I checked. But something's gone wrong."

"I will be the judge of that." They hurried down the corridor past the nursery.

At the door to the ward, Steve stood bewildered, searching for that one beloved form.

"This way."

There she is. Lila!

She lay without moving, hair tousled on the pillow, like a worn baby doll. No sounds, no smiles, nor even frowns hinted at what was happening inside. The sheet rose and fell slightly—once, twice, without a regular rhythm.

"Leave." The young doctor's pleasant expression darkened. "I must examine Mrs. Romero."

"I'm her husband. I want to stay." Steve's voice croaked in protest.

"Not now." Compassion lent an authority to the doctor's voice that Steve couldn't ignore. "Go back to the waiting room. I will talk with you when I have completed my examination." With a gentle push, he steered Steve toward the door and pulled the curtain around the silent bed.

"Let's go." Carrie slipped a cool hand into Steve's and led him away. "The doctor is here. He'll know what to do." Their shoes echoed on the linoleum floor, her sneakers squeaking against the tiles while his loafers tapped with a hesitant beat.

Tim met them at the door, eyes asking the questions he didn't voice. Steve shook his head and began pacing the floor.

Out of habit, he counted the steps like he did for band routines. *Thirty strides, turn right, thirty-five more steps, turn, complete the circuit. Two minutes.* He circled again, studying the pictures of dignitaries on the wall—ten of them, including one he recognized as President Iliescu. A dark rectangular space marked the place where a frame had been removed. Ceausescu, probably. Steve continued pacing a third then fourth round.

Carrie walked toward him, bearing a steaming mug. "I thought you might like some coffee. Probably strong enough to tar a ship, but it might help." She tucked her head to one side and held the cup in the palm of her hand as an offering, for the moment resembling a shy young band student.

"Thanks." The heat stung Steve's hand briefly when he grasped the cup. He stopped his pacing long enough to take a sip. She was right; it was strong. The sweet syrupy coffee soothed his throat, enabling him to voice the fears that tormented him.

"He said a few minutes." Flicking his wrist, a luminous dial shone against dark matted hair. "It's already been a quarter of an hour. What's going on in there?" *Stop shouting.*

His voice echoed around the nearly empty anteroom. A couple in the corner looked up at the noise then shrugged at the strange Americans.

Warily, like kittens sidling up to a bulldog, Tim and Pastor Radu joined Steve and Carrie. Tim hugged his brother-in-law, a brief, awkward gesture meant to encourage.

"It will be all right. Remember God is in control." Tim gently punched Steve's shoulder. "I've reached Brenda back in the States. She'll let the family know." He smiled as if to say, "That's that. Things will work out. You'll see."

They stood in a tight circle, Steve trembling from the effort it took to not start pacing again. He sank in a chair, hung his head low, and dangled his hands between his knees.

Lord. The uncertain cry issued straight from his heart. *I don't know how to pray. My feelings are too strong. But I trust You with the lives of my wife and our baby. I trust You to do what is best.*

Metal rattled as someone turned a door handle. Steve jumped to his feet. The doctor appeared in the doorway, blinking his eyes against the dark waiting room.

"Mr. Romero?"

He sprinted to the door, vaguely aware of the others at his heels. "How's Lila?"

"Let's find a place to sit down. Back here." The doctor

pushed through a swinging door and settled at a desk behind the receptionist's spot. The shadowy light and black bags under his eyes added years to his face.

The doctor tapped a pencil on the desktop, as if stalling for time, then opened a drawer and rolled it in. Folding his hands together, he looked Steve straight in the eye.

"Mrs. Romero is in a coma. We're not sure what caused it."

Coma? "What can you do?"

The doctor continued as if he hadn't heard Steve. "Her heart is skipping beats. She is having trouble breathing—we are trying to locate a machine."

He spread his hands as if in apology. "You must make a choice. We can take extraordinary measures to try to bring Mrs. Romero out of the coma and hope she recovers quickly."

The words pounded in Steve's brain. *Choice? What choice? Save her!*

"What is the other option?" Tim asked for him.

"The longer you wait, the more danger there is to the baby. He is not receiving enough oxygen—he could die, or have unexpected disabilities. If we do a cesarean now, there is a good chance he will be born healthy."

"Then what would happen to my wife?"

"Mr. Romero, I will not lie to you. She will probably die if we perform an operation. She may die even if we don't."

Steve didn't need time to consider. "Save my wife." The words came out with a harsh, grating edge. Lila! Without her, a child, a family, meant nothing.

"Very well." The doctor stood up, ending the conference. Steve tried to follow him back into the ward. "No." The doctor warned him away in brisk tones. "You would only be a distraction. You might slow us down." Compassion softened the next words. "I will let you know as soon as anything changes." The door clanged shut behind him like a maximum-security prison.

One hour passed. Two. Three. Periodically a nurse slipped through the door and shook her head—no change. Steve resumed his pacing. Outside the glass doors, an angry red-and-orange sky announced the dawn of a new day.

Steve had lost all track of time when the doctor reappeared. The doctor's lab coat fell in dejected folds around his sagging body.

"She's dead." Steve spoke in a strangled voice.

The doctor nodded his head. "A blood clot went to the brain. Nothing we could do. We went ahead and took the baby."

"Is the baby alive? A boy? A girl?" Steve asked automatically. The news of Lila's death spread through his body, numbing nerve endings in its wake.

"You have a son, Mr. Romero. But there are problems."

The edge in the doctor's voice penetrated the fog clogging Steve's brain. "Problems?"

"He is premature, of course. Small and not fully developed. His lungs are not functioning properly. I believe there may be a problem with his heart valves as well. And only time will determine how much brain damage he suffered."

"Will he—live?"

The doctor's helpless shrug spoke volumes. "We are doing the best we can."

"Please—let me see them. I can't get in the way now." Steve's voice nearly broke.

"This way."

The doctor didn't object when Tim and Carrie followed Steve down the hallway. Empty stillness screamed in Steve's ears from where Lila's body lay on the bed, sheets drawn up past her shoulders. He stood at her side, smoothed her hair back from her face. *She's gone. All that's left is this shell. "Absent from the body, present with the Lord." No, God, not like this!* He started to cry, but the pervading numbness dried up his tear ducts.

"Where is my son?"

The doctor guided them to the nursery and pointed to a bassinet in a far corner. Half a dozen tubes hid the tiny body. A T-line from an oxygen tank, like Steve had seen hundreds of times in Denver, obscured the baby's facial features. In spite of the oxygen, his skin shone bluish-white, not healthy newborn red. Steve reached for the baby, but his arms ran into the glass. He hung there like a fly caught in a spider's web.

Tim tapped him on the elbow. Tears glistened in his eyes. "I'm sorry, man. We've got to go—fill the group in on what's happened, cancel tonight's concert. But I'll be back."

Next to him, Carrie pressed her face against the glass, tears leaving a salty streak on the pane. "What's his name?"

"Huh?" Steve tried to focus on her question.

"What's the baby's name? So that I can pray for him."

"Brandon. That's what we finally decided." Soundless sobs shook his shoulders. A featherlight hand touched his back then disappeared.

Steve continued staring into the nursery. His plans and hopes for the future lay struggling on a nursery bed, reduced to a single thin note.

three

With sandpapered eyes, Carrie stared out the taxi window. Bucharest greeted a new day. Newspaper boys and milk vendors called cheerful greetings as they went about their business in the light morning sun. Life continued as usual—no cosmic pause commemorated the death of an unknown American or the child's life hanging in the balance. Unbidden sobs rose in her throat.

"Carrie." Tim's voice interrupted her thoughts. "Thanks for being there."

"I can't believe she's gone. We only met a week ago, but I really liked her."

"Not what you expected from Romania. A disaster for the tour. And Steve—if it was my wife, I'd go crazy."

They passed the Palace of the People. Beggars dotted the steps, visible symbols of communism's unfulfilled promises. "Only last night Lila was talking about this place." Carrie's heart contracted. *It just can't be. I wish I could wake up and find out it's all been a bad dream.* She closed her eyes, wanting to shut out the nightmare.

The taxi jolted to a stop. They had arrived at the hotel. Neon signs flashed as if it were still the dead of night. She began to cry.

"Go on up," Tim urged gently. "Try to get some sleep. We'll meet in the lobby at nine thirty." Shoulders hunched over in apparent exhaustion, he headed for the phones.

Of course. He has to let the families know, thought Carrie, as she shuffled off in the opposite direction.

Fatigue overtook Carrie at the staircase. To her tired mind, the steps had multiplied overnight to rival the climb she made the previous week at the Statue of Liberty. Wishing she could crawl or propel herself forward by her arms, she lifted one heavy leg after the other in slow progression. Each step became a resting place to stand while she checked her pockets for the room key and to catch her breath.

The room. Remembering the mess they had left, Carrie hesitated before opening the door. Nothing had changed. The middle of the bed sagged under the roll of wet bedspreads. She checked her watch. 7:00 a.m. *Too early for the maid.* Loud ticking emanated from Lila's travel alarm. Once again Carrie felt the sensation of waking up in a soaking-wet bed, the panic, and excitement, too, of Lila going into labor.

Sleep if you can. Tim said nine thirty. She reset the alarm. *But where do I sleep?* Stifling a groan, Carrie turned the one cushiony chair toward the wall, curled herself up as small as she could in its depths, and tried to sleep. Sunlight leaked through the window shade, warming her back and relaxing tense muscles.

Lila's in trouble. I've got to help her! Aaah!

The alarm blared by Carrie's ear. She jerked awake, sliding out of the chair onto the floor. A musty, wet smell filled the air. *It's real. Lila is dead.* She checked the clock—nine twenty. *I'd better hurry.*

A few minutes later Carrie made her way to the lobby, where Pastor Radu greeted her. Daylight hours revealed a friendly, round face. An inner peace transformed his rather ordinary features. He took her hands between his own and patted them with thick, blunt fingers. "I am so sorry. It is sometimes difficult to understand God's workings."

Memories of stories about Radu's heroism surfaced. Tortured at the hands of communists, he refused to deny his faith. *And he still talks about God's love.* She hoped to get to know him better.

Maybe I can ask Tim about Steve. She saw the director conversing in low tones with one of the older tour members. Flipping through her memory banks, she placed him as Guy, the trumpeter who could make his instrument sing like the archangel Michael. *No, I shouldn't intrude.* She sagged against the wall to wait for an announcement.

Curious glances shot in her direction then looked away, unwilling to meet her eyes. Whispers circulated around her like strings of fog. Every now and then the words penetrated the wall of silence surrounding her.

"Lila. . .in labor."

"I heard she died."

"No, Steve died. . .car accident."

"Everyone's fine. . .Lila had a boy."

"Carrie went with them. . . ."

Heads swung in her direction like a pendulum swing.

"I'll ask." A determined Amy Knight headed toward her, ready to voice their questions.

"Your attention, please." Tim's announcement saved her from having to answer. "Singers. Let's load the bus." In spite of his measured control, cracks showed in his razor-edge hold on reality.

No one moved. "Not everybody's here." Amy spoke for the group. "Steve and Lila are missing." The proverbial pin-drop silence descended.

"I know." Tim paused, looking at the bustle going on around them. "I'd rather not talk about it here. I'll explain what happened in a few minutes, at the church. Let's go."

Guy picked up his instrument case and headed out the door. One by one, others followed. An uneasy silence pervaded. Carrie groped her way to the back, unwilling to join in idle chitchat or to offer explanations. At the front Tim scrunched over his seat as if he were experiencing motion sickness. Radu took the seat next to him. No one dared to sit close to either one of them. Currents of muffled whispers eddied through the bus.

Eventually they arrived at the church, a cathedral with gothic spires worthy of a vampire movie. A banner hung across the front entrance. "Welcome to Romania." The unintended cruelty stung Carrie's eyes. *Some welcome we've had.*

Radu motioned them inside. Carrie paused for a moment to stare at a painting of a huge tree that dominated one wall. *Tree of Jesse.* Her mind dragged up the relevant description from the tourist information she had studied. Then she joined the others shuffling toward the front.

Tim grabbed a mike, flicked a switch, and waited for everyone to find a seat.

"Amy, you asked earlier about Steve and Lila." Each word resonated in a voice full of pathos. He surveyed the room, found Carrie, and looked at her as if seeking a way to put the night's tragedy into words. "The baby started coming last night. Early, as you know. We rushed Lila to the hospital, but she went into a coma, and a blood clot hit her brain and killed her. They're trying to save the baby now, and Steve is at the hospital with him." The words tumbled out quickly, as if rushing through the explanation could minimize their impact.

Shock held them silent for a moment; then the questions started. "Lila's dead?"

Tim nodded his head without uttering a word.

"And the baby—it's a boy?"

"Brandon." Carrie surprised herself by speaking. "His name is Brandon." The image of the tiny infant, tied to life by dozens of tubes, formed in her mind, choking further speech.

"How is Steve?"

"In shock, as you might imagine. He needs your prayers."

"Is the tour canceled?"

Half of Carrie's mind struggled to pay attention.

"We've canceled the concert scheduled for this evening, but the tour will go on with a modified schedule." He fielded a few more questions, expanding on the same information, letting it sink in. "Guy will lead today's rehearsal. Ask Radu for anything else you need." He started to bolt out the door when the Romanian stopped him.

"Let us pray." The pastor turned toward the altar and raised his arms in supplication. "Our loving heavenly Father, we pray for Your children Lila, Steve, and little Brandon. We do not ask for life but for peace and joy. We accept that Your will be done." *He prays as if he's talking to God over the breakfast table.*

When he finished, Tim took charge. "Join hands in a circle." Confidence and joy built in his voice as he prayed. "Lord Jesus, You have promised You are with us always. You called Lila home. We confess we don't understand, but we know You are with Steve and Brandon right now. We will go on, knowing You have given us the victory in Your Son Jesus Christ! Amen!"

The group waited in silence, continuing to hold hands when Tim concluded. Guy began praying. "Jesus. We need You today more than ever. . . ."

One by one they prayed, offering broken hearts to God with faith and love. Carrie added her unspoken thoughts to those of the others. *He is here,* she realized, feeling the presence of the Holy Spirit in an almost physical sense as if dove wings brushed her face. Peace erased part of the pain she had carried away from the hospital.

After what could have been minutes or hours, the sobs diminished and the circle broke. Tim had disappeared. Carrie guessed he'd headed back to the hospital.

In a few minutes the group assembled in the choir loft, everyone careful not to stare at the empty spot in the alto section and the unoccupied piano bench. Guy called for their attention.

"Can anyone fill in at the piano?" He gestured toward the empty seat. "Tim usually plays when Steve can't make it." He swallowed. "I know there must be at least one piano major out there."

"Kim plays for our college choir," one of the tenors offered.

"Just what we're looking for. Come on down, Kim. Don't be shy." Carrie twisted to watch a willowy redhead slip out of the back row.

The instrumentalists did their best—they all did—but heavy hearts and a different blend of voices and instruments took a toll. To Carrie's ears, their singing lacked balance. Lunch call came two hours later.

"All right, wrap it up for this morning." Guy sounded as relieved as Carrie felt.

Pastor Radu's wife, Anika, served a Romanian specialty in honor of their arrival, but Carrie ate it without appreciation. *Comfort food, that's what I want. A hot fudge brownie sundae. A supreme pizza. Has Steve eaten anything today?* She remembered Lila, who would never again enjoy a meal, and the food turned sour in her mouth.

❧

Brandon's tiny lips moved in a sucking motion. *He's hungry.* The bag delivering the life-sustaining fluids dangled, empty.

"Nurse!" Language barrier forgotten for the moment, Steve called for help. When no one responded, he raced down the hall to where the matron, a different lady from the previous evening, kept watch over the nursery.

"Nurse. My son's food bag is empty. . . ." She looked at him, puzzled. He tried to think of a way to pantomime the problem and gave up. "Come with me. Please."

Shrugging, she set aside the knitting that had occupied her attention and followed him through the maze of cribs. "Look. It's empty." He pointed to the collapsed bag.

On the way out, a couple of babies started whimpering. She checked her watch and lifted them from their beds. *Lucky kids. Strong enough to cry. Mothers here to feed them.* Angry, he listened as a feeble mewling noise issued from Brandon's mouth. *He belongs in a neonatal care unit.* Powerless fury at the inefficient, unfamiliar Romanian system washed over Steve.

Five minutes passed. The nurse returned empty-handed. She pointed to an empty spot in the cabinet. Moving with a minimum of effort, she retrieved an empty bottle from a sterilization unit and extracted formula from a refrigerator. She looked at Steve, asking a question with her eyes.

He nodded, and she poured about two ounces into the bottle before handing it to him. It felt cold in his hands. "Uh, is there any way to warm it? Microwave?" She stared at him blankly and gestured toward Brandon, inviting Steve to feed his son.

I can't give him cold formula. Steve's mind fished for a solution. Hot water, maybe? Worth a try. He turned the tap on at the sink. Thankfully the rusty water cleared and warmed to near boiling point. He stuck the bottle under the running water, frantic to get the formula ready before Brandon reached a critical point. At least the chill had disappeared. He scurried to Brandon's side.

The baby's mouth sucked frantically, searching instinctively for food. Weaving his hand carefully through the tubing, Steve offered the nipple to his son. Tiny gulping noises followed. *I hope this is all right. There must have been a reason for the IV.* Steve shoved the worries aside as Brandon's cries subsided, followed by small mewing sounds of contentment. Steve could almost see the nourishment filling out hollow cheeks.

Feeding wasn't supposed to be a problem. Inspired by the doctor's advice and Brenda's example, Lila had planned on nursing their child. *Lila! How can I raise our child without you?*

I don't have time to think about that now. Pushing the grief into a locked corner of his heart, he gently extracted the nipple from Brandon's mouth. *Who's going to burp him?* Warming a bottle was a simple obstacle to overcome. Would his lungs ever inflate and function properly? Brandon's chest heaved in the effort to breath in air. *God, he has to make it. He just has to.*

❧

Carrie managed a few more bites of lunch by washing them down with a glass of lemon-lime soda. She turned her attention to the Tree of Jesse on the wall. The fresco fascinated her. Not quite symmetrical limbs branched out from a thick trunk. Portraits of biblical characters hung from the luxuriant leaves. David held a lamb. The boy Josiah wore a crown. Atop the tree, a radiant Madonna cradled the baby Jesus in soft blankets.

Brandon. The IV lines that wrapped the tiny infant curled into Carrie's mind, and she wiped at her eyes. Grief washed over her afresh, and she stabbed a fork through a paper napkin and pushed away her plate. *This can't be real. Lord, be with Steve and Brandon.*

"I see you admire the Tree of Jesse." Pastor Radu addressed her. "So do I. I always notice some new thing. It reminds me that God became man, and He knows our weaknesses." He pointed to the infant Christ. "Even the Lord of heaven knew loss—Joseph. His good friend Lazarus." A peculiar light shone from his eyes. "But because He lives, we can face tomorrow. Isn't that what the song says?"

A newborn baby. Brandon. God does understand.

Radu smiled encouragement at her then tapped his glass for attention. "For those who wish to go, we have planned a sightseeing trip this afternoon. Or you may return to the hotel." He outlined some traditional tourist hot spots Carrie had included on her must-see list. *Does it matter now?* In light of Lila's death, everything diminished in importance.

"There may be other things you want to see." Radu was still speaking. "Let me know, and I will try to arrange something."

Surely they won't keep us in Bucharest indefinitely. Maybe she could escape the horror of the night and find a gentler Romania in the countryside. Her hunger sharpened for an excursion down the Danube River or up into the Carpathian Mountains.

But what about today? I'm exhausted. I feel like I could sleep all afternoon and night, too. She remembered the soiled sheets rolled in the middle of the bed. The maid must have cleaned up the mess, but Carrie was sure she couldn't rest with reminders of the previous evening surrounding her. Before bedtime she would try to change rooms. *Maybe sightseeing will take my mind off things.* Most of the group climbed on the bus with her.

Pastor Radu proved a relaxing tour guide. From time to time he passed on bits of history and culture, but as often as not he let the sights speak for themselves. Colorful clothing sparkled against gray buildings, differing styles separating Romanians from Hungarians from Gypsies. She had heard racial tensions rivaled those in the United States. *In Christ there is no Jew nor Greek.* Carrie studied Pastor Radu and his wife, the love of Christ radiating from their faces. *Language doesn't matter. We have the same Father.*

Catching sight of a mother surrounded by half a dozen youngsters, Carrie decided that large families must be the norm in Romania. Everywhere she saw children. Mothers stood in line with five or six pale-faced tots clinging to their skirts. The lucky ones bounced a ball in the street or ran laughing through a park. What had she heard about a government-dictated baby boom? Thousands of children crowded into space designed for hundreds.

Watching them, Carrie knew exactly where she wanted to go on the next day. She made her way forward on the wildly swinging bus and tapped Pastor Radu on the shoulder.

"*Buna dimineata,* Carrie. How are you doing?"

"Okay, I guess." She braced herself against the back of the seat and spoke. "I know what I want to do tomorrow, if you can arrange it." She hesitated. *What if he thinks I'm foolish? Pushy?*

"Yes?" he prompted.

"I want to visit an orphanage. You know, a home for children."

His face registered surprise. *At least he didn't say no.* "You see, I'm a social work major. I plan on working with children in some way."

"I see," he murmured. Anika looked on with surprised interest.

"And we've heard so much about the orphans in Romania. I'd like to see for myself." She almost didn't dare look at him, afraid of his response.

"You remind me of Solomon," he said in a seeming change of subject.

Me? Solomon? How?

"You ask for knowledge to help when you could ask for pleasure. You are a special person. A children's home—" He paused, as if flipping through mental files.

"Sister Pauline," his wife murmured.

"Of course!" Radu said. "We know someone who runs a home. We may be able to arrange something."

"Thank you!" Carrie shook his hand and raced back to her seat before he changed his mind. Her head settled against the hard red seat, and she dozed off and on through the remainder of the tour.

Back at the hotel, Carrie wasted no time eating, changing rooms, and settling in for a long night's sleep. Fighting yawns, she said a brief but heartfelt prayer for the father and son struggling at the hospital. She'd half expected visions of the previous evening to keep her awake, but three sleep-shortened nights took their toll. The instant her head hit the pillow, she fell into a drug-deep sleep.

During the next morning's breakfast, served American style with eggs, bacon, orange juice, and toast, Carrie wondered what the children in the orphanage were eating. *Probably not much*, she thought, guiltily laying down her fork on a not yet empty plate. *God bless all the hungry children everywhere. The ones in the orphanage. And Brandon, whatever is happening with him today.*

Pastor Radu's wife, Anika, walked into the dining room. She stood by the doorway, surveying the room until she spotted Carrie.

Anika joined Carrie at the table. "Can you leave immediately? Sister Pauline can see you this morning."

Yes! Then Carrie noticed Guy making his way around the tables. "I don't know yet. I hope so. I have to check with the leader." He headed in their direction.

"Good morning, Mrs. Babik," Guy greeted Anika. He looked a little bewildered, like an understudy called on as the curtain rises. "Carrie, I thought I'd let you know the schedule. Today's another free day. Tim is making arrangements to ship Lila's body home. Whatever happens with Steve and the baby, Tim will rejoin us tomorrow. Plan on a ten o'clock rehearsal in the morning." With a brief wave of his hand, he moved on to the next group.

Brandon must still be alive, Carrie realized, gratitude swelling her heart like lighter-than-air helium. *Thank You, Lord. Help Steve through this difficult time.* There was nothing more she could do for Lila. Children always cheered her up. Maybe visiting the orphanage would take her mind off the tragedy. She folded her napkin and laid it on top of her plate.

"I'm ready. Let's go!"

four

"Let's go." Tim steered Steve away from the crib and out of the nursery. "Man, you have to get some shut-eye. The hospital will call if anything changes."

Through the distorted glass, Brandon lay still, almost lifeless. Steve blinked hard, trying to flush moisture over exhaustion-dried eyes. He fought the urge to run back. Surely Tim understood his fear that the only phone call he would receive would be about a dead child.

"I know you're worried. I booked you a room in a hotel down the block. You can hole up there and be back in five minutes. I promise."

Steve couldn't tear himself away from the window.

"You're not doing the baby or yourself any good, carrying on like this."

Maybe a short nap. Steve's shoulders sagged, and he ran the back of his hand across his bristly chin. He hadn't changed clothes for almost twenty-four hours. A hotel room beckoned as a haven of rest to his weary mind. Turning his back on the nursery window, he followed Tim down the hall.

The planned nap lasted all night. When he woke, gentle pink light filtered around the edges of the window shades. Grabbing the phone, he dialed the front desk.

"This is Steve Romero in suite 116. Has the hospital called?"

"No, sir."

Thank goodness he speaks English.

"We would have called right away."

Maybe I have time for that shower after all. He stayed under the nozzle until it turned ice cold, the water stinging his back like needles. It was like a form of acupuncture, each jab removing a minuscule amount of the pain of the last two days. His mind cleared, and he realized he probably should contact the American embassy. They could advise him about what to do about a funeral and burial.

Wiping the mist off the bathroom mirror, he stared at his image, a gaunt-faced stranger looking back at him. Nothing to invite anyone to want to help him. *First impressions are important.* Tim's advice to the Singers echoed through his head with Lila's voice. Grimly he slapped shaving cream on his cheeks and starting scraping off two days' growth of beard.

He had just fastened his shirt cuffs, easily pushing the button through the loose hole, when someone knocked at the door. "Come in."

Tim appeared and looked him up and down. "You rested. That's good."

Steve grunted.

"My next job is to get some food into you."

"No time for that. I want to contact the American embassy. When will the hospital release Lila's body?"

"I've already called." Tim polished his glasses then pushed them up onto his nose. "You'll have to sign some papers. It may take a few days. Breakfast now. No more excuses."

Steve allowed Tim to guide him to the hotel's dining room while he considered the problem of the interment. "The only funeral home I know anything about is Drinkwine Mortuary. It stuck in my mind because the name was kind of unusual, you know? We don't—didn't—have any burial plots." He swallowed, hard. "Or a will. We thought we had plenty of time."

In the restaurant, Steve was glad that the menu listed the selections in Romanian and English. Tim shoveled in the food in his usual impatient fashion, while Steve picked at the meal, not tasting the little he managed to swallow. He couldn't have told anyone if the eggs were reconstituted powder or fresh from the farm.

"Brenda is calling our church back home. The minister will arrange things on the Denver end." Tim settled back, coffee cup cradled between his hands, a pose Steve had seen hundreds of times. "Yeah, Brenda and I didn't get around to making a will until after Amanda was born. We even joked about it. How it made us feel like old married folks. Never imagined anyone our age needing it." He took a sip and glanced at Steve over the rim of the cup.

"Man, I feel so bad about what's happened. If Lila hadn't been on tour—"

"If, if, if." Anger crept into Steve's voice. "If we had been in Denver. If they had better facilities here. It wouldn't have made any difference. Lila might have died, even with the best of care. Nothing can change what's happened." The tears Steve had held in check tumbled out, cascading down his clean shirt, leaving streaks like the slats on a baby crib.

At his elbow Steve heard liquid being poured into a cup, and he forced himself to stop crying.

Tim handed him a wet napkin to clean his face and waited while Steve drank down his coffee. "Are you ready to go back to the hospital?"

"Yeah, I guess so."

"We can wait a few more minutes—"

Outside the window a passing cloud dimmed the morning sunshine. "No. I want to see my son."

❧

Carrie squeezed into the battered two-seater, making room between a pile of Bibles and a box of pamphlets. Anika handled the manual gears as smoothly as a race car, dodging the bumps Carrie thought unavoidable after her rides by taxi and bus. Bright sunlight created an illusion of prosperity in the passing residential districts.

"Radu tells me you were with Mrs. Romero at the hospital," Anika stated. "It must have been frightening." Her tone invited a response.

Carrie blinked. *How can I tell this stranger the way I felt when I don't know myself? I've never seen anyone die before. It was so sudden, like when someone pinches out the flame of a candle.* Although no breeze stirred the stale car air, she shivered.

"It was pretty frightening," she admitted.

"That took courage. Helping Mr. and Mrs. Romero even when you were scared." The admiration in Anika's voice shook Carrie.

I wasn't brave at all. I butted in, wanted to be the aunt. And I couldn't help Lila when she needed me most. Memories of Lila lying still on the bed filled her mind and choked further speech.

"Ah, here we are." The car turned onto a tree-lined lane.

Good. I need to hear children's laughter.

"The home is on the Dimbovita River. It used to be a pretty spot." She pulled into a parking space in front of an ancient building. At some point in the distant past it was a stately country home, since converted into an orphanage. Everywhere signs of neglect showed, from ivy climbing up crumbling brick walls to weatherworn slides and swings at the side in need of fresh paint.

Carrie stepped out of the car, breathed in the fresh air, and smiled. *What a wonderful place for kids.* Peering down the lane, she saw no sign of the children she expected.

To the right four more buildings, each more institutional in design than the last, crowded together. Small square windows occurred at regular intervals in the last two buildings, both three stories high. *It looks like a jail,* Carrie thought with a shock.

"This way." Anika lifted the door knocker with effort. *It*

was old and gloomy enough that Carrie half expected Jacob Marley's face to appear. A minute passed. Two.

"Do you think they heard us?" Carrie asked, impatient, grasping the heavy ring in her fingers.

"Yes." Anika gently pushed away Carrie's hand. "Sister Pauline is old. It may take her a few minutes."

Patience, Carrie reminded herself. *Remember Tim's advice.*

The door opened by unseen hands. Carrie spied a skeleton-thin woman with fluttering hands and lively blue eyes.

Anika spoke briefly in Romanian, gesturing to Carrie.

"Buna dimineata." A dove soft voice transported Carrie back in time. Her kindergarten teacher had spoken with the same gentle nurturing tones. *I like this woman.* A warm reassurance engulfed her.

Sister Pauline led them down the hall lined with sturdy furniture in need of polishing, past black-and-white photographs of rosy-cheeked children with bright smiles and old-fashioned clothes. Carrie stopped to study one picture. *Isn't that. . . ? It is!* A younger Sister Pauline, hair black, not gray, shoulders straight and not yet bent, peered at her with the same piercing eyes. *She's given her life to this place.*

"Sister Pauline speaks no English, so I will translate," Anika explained when they settled in the office.

Carrie watched the evident enthusiasm and joy on the director's face as she spoke of her early days with the home. There were always children, those orphaned by violence and circumstance, babies born to unwed mothers.

She's like me. A smile of camaraderie broke Carrie's face. *God called her to help "the least of these."*

The number of new workers diminished with the communist takeover, but they managed. Pauline became the director twenty-five years ago.

"For years, love and children filled our home." Happy

memories eased some of the life lines of her face as she described life in the converted mansion.

One home? But there are five buildings.

"That changed with Ceausescu." Sadness etched furrows in the older woman's forehead. The government assessed a celibacy tax on women with fewer than five children and outlawed contraception. It quickly made a difference. The birth rate nearly doubled in only one year's time. At first, it wasn't bad. Families could absorb their increasing numbers. Only after exceeding normal resources did parents start turning to the orphanage in hopes that their children would receive better care.

"Soon we had to build a second home. Three more followed in quick succession, gradually replacing a homelike atmosphere with institutional efficiency. No new workers came to help with the ever-increasing number of children. We are growing old, you see, and there are not enough of us." Tears pooled in the corners of Sister Pauline's eyes. "One worker has to take care of forty babies. Forty!" She looked at a picture of Jesus blessing the children. "Lord, forgive us." She wiped away her tears. "At least with Ceausescu and the communists gone, now they can be baptized."

Before they die. The unspoken words hung in the air like clouds pregnant with rain.

I don't want to hear any more. And I haven't even seen the children yet. At her side, Anika stirred.

"Do you want to go on?" A gentle hand brushed her arm.

I don't want to. But I have to. Slowly Carrie nodded.

"God bless." Sister Pauline's peaceful smile conveyed her meaning before Anika translated. Rising from her chair to her full height that barely reached Carrie's shoulder, she hugged her with surprising strength. "Cristina will show you around." She pulled a bell rope.

Minutes passed. *Another opportunity to exercise patience.* Carrie took the opportunity to study the office. Floor-to-ceiling bookcases lined two walls, and pictures filled the back wall like the bulletin board at her old pediatrician's office. On her right, worn toys overflowed from a box. To the left, a thick volume that could only be a Bible lay open on a prayer bench where the varnish had worn off.

In the hall, shuffling noises indicated the arrival of their guide. A middle-aged woman shambled toward them, and Carrie guessed at her Down's syndrome before she saw the telltale eyes. *Is this who takes care of the children?*

"Cristina has lived here all her life," Anika said as if sensing Carrie's question. "We're the only family she has. She helps in the kitchen and the laundry."

Sister Pauline talked briefly with the woman and moved from behind the desk to bid them good-bye. As they headed out the door, Carrie saw her kneeling by the prayer bench.

First Cristina led them to her domain, the laundry rooms and kitchens. Her face shone with pride as she demonstrated the assembly-line efficiency of preparing one hundred bottles at once. "For the babies." She cradled her arms and rocked to make sure Carrie understood.

"Yes, very nice." Carrie's mind boggled at the prospect. *What did Sister Pauline say? One worker to forty babies? And five were too many for me at the church nursery!*

Next she led through a long corridor.

"I think she wants to show you to the nurse's office." Anika explained their next destination. "They have a modern facility. A group of French doctors donated the equipment. Dr. Reynaud visits every two months or so."

Carrie checked her watch. Noon was approaching, and her stomach was rumbling. *Where are the children?* Turning to Anika, she asked, "Can we skip it for now? I'd like to see the wards. Please."

"Of course." Anika spoke with Cristina. Turning away from the lab with slow reluctance, she hoisted a full basket and walked with a shambling gait toward the farthest building. She opened the door on a dark, musty hallway.

Silence reigned. Not a toy nor a peep hinted at the presence of children nearby. Had Cristina misunderstood the request?

"Where are the children?"

"Right here." Anika opened another door. A woman, older than Sister Pauline, sat looking through a wall-length glass partition.

She can't possibly take care of the children by herself. A nagging doubt suggested she probably did. Carrie moved to where she could see through the window.

The room stretched as long as half a football field. Beds crowded together in clusters of four. Through the thin glass, Carrie heard the faint slapping of feet on the floor. Here and there she spotted a few brave adventurers, maybe half a dozen, walking and crawling along the linoleum. Some children poked noses through the crib railings, watching the movement with unblinking gazes.

"How old are they?" Despite their small size, they didn't seem to be infants. Anika translated, and Cristina held up three fingers.

Three years old? And still crawling?

"This is Marie." Anika introduced the elderly woman. "She will you take in."

Clamor like a dynamite blast broke the silence as soon as she opened the door. Children swarmed toward Marie and Carrie. Voices desperate for a second of attention cried, "Mama! Mama!" The sister bent over as far as her clearly arthritic back would allow, touching hair and fingers.

She paused for a second by each crib, calling the children by name and bestowing kisses or smiles on their drawn faces.

Here and there a scrap of cloth, a well-worn doll, added a touch of color to the white-on-white cribs. Carrie thought of the riot of spring that adorned her home church's nursery—fitted crib sheets, rail bumpers, baby animals gamboling along the walls.

New sound pounded into her consciousness. Across the room, red streaked down the peeling paint where a boy banged his head against the wall. *Autostimulation.* She gulped.

Marie slowly crossed the room, lifted the child into her arms, and hugged him for a moment before she cleaned the blood from his forehead. Carrie turned her attention away, unwilling to watch.

A girl with pretty blond curls blinked at her with crossed eyes. Out of habit, Carrie initiated a game of peekaboo. She hid her face behind her hands then snatched them away. The child looked at her with the same fixed gaze, no giggle or glimmer of a smile suggesting she enjoyed the game.

Maybe she didn't see me. Carrie leaned over the crib and tried again. The child lifted a thin arm toward Carrie, dropped it, and resumed her cross-eyed study of the ceiling.

In the next crib, a boy quietly rocked himself, thumb in mouth. He also ignored Carrie's attempts at play. *I feel invisible.* The children reminded her of an experiment she had read about. Baby chimpanzees were divided into two groups. Both groups had every physical need provided. However, adults played only with one group. The second group, without that additional social nurturing, wasted away and failed to thrive.

As thin and pale as the children were, Carrie doubted if their basic living needs were adequate. Some of them looked as emaciated as famine victims from Africa. She jumped, startled, as twig-thin fingers wrapped themselves around hers.

"Hi, Miron." Anika kissed the top of his head. "I know him. An American couple almost adopted him last year."

"Almost? What happened?" Carrie stared at his black eyes and sunken cheeks.

"He has AIDS." Anika said it as casually as if she had announced he was left-handed.

Carrie pulled her hand away as if Anika had said sulfuric acid. "AIDS?" The words stumbled out in disbelief.

"Yes." Anika sighed. "For a time, babies were given blood transfusions when they were born. Doctors thought it would make them stronger. Unfortunately, some of the blood supply was tainted. And little ones like Miron are sick."

Carrie turned on her heels, suddenly angry—at Ceausescu, for causing hurt to so many parents, at parents who could not or would not care for their own, at an orphanage that barely provided for physical needs. *I'm even angry at You, God. Why do You let these innocent ones suffer?* Shutting her senses to the children, she bolted through the door.

❧

One black eye squinted at Steve, like every baby picture he had ever seen. *He looks perfect, a miniature human being.* His nose curled a bit to one side like Sammy's did when he was born. His ears hugged the side of his face, like Lila's had. A shock of dark hair stuck out at angles from his head.

Eyes, ears, nose—all accounted for. Ten toes and fingers. *Long, pianist's fingers—like mine. "It's not fair," Brenda used to complain. "I can barely reach an octave."*

He's perfect on the outside. My son—and Lila's. Steve's heart tightened in his chest. "He's beautiful, honey," he whispered. "But he wasn't ready yet."

The problems lurked inside. Brandon's lungs couldn't draw in enough air. His heart valves hadn't completely closed. Only God knew how much brain damage had occurred during childbirth.

My son. Steve looked at Brandon, gasping for air beneath

the oxygen mask. Tears welled in his eyes. He brushed them away angrily. "If only I could hold you."

"Let him go, Steve," a voice inside him urged. "He still needs his mother. Let him join her."

Tears flowed down Steve's cheeks. "Just a few more days, Lord," he begged. "Even one more day." He collapsed, weeping, beside the crib.

❧

The last day, Carrie mused as sunshine beat down on her back. *Sand, sea, and sunshine today, concert tonight, flight home tomorrow. I'm ready to leave Romania behind.* Rays strong enough to blot out the ugly memories of the hospital and of the orphanage warmed her winter-white skin. She slapped sunscreen on her exposed arms and legs and turned over.

The original two days of rest in Constanta by the Black Sea had been cut in half because of a revised tour schedule. *One day is better than none.* It came as a welcome relief after ten days of constant travel and performance. *Good times follow bad as surely as sunshine follows rain.*

What will I remember most about Romania? Those frightful first forty-eight hours or the last ten days? Already she had forgotten details, like the color of the linoleum at the hospital.

One thing was certain, Steve would never forget. He waited in Bucharest, until Brandon was strong enough to travel. If he ever would be. *Bring them both home safe and sound. And if that doesn't happen—help Steve through this terrible time.*

Flicking sand off her feet, she glanced at her watch. Two o'clock—there was time for one last dip before dressing for the concert. Currents of memories crossed her mind as she floated weightless in the warm salt water. Tim directing from the piano. Singing solo one night. Her onetime jealousy of Amy. Daily bulletins on Brandon's progress. Plans for a memorial service for Lila. Half an hour later she emerged from the water, dried off, and slipped into her sandals.

"Carrie, wait up." Kim and Amy ran toward her. "Have you heard the news?" Their faces were serious.

"No. What's happened?" *Brandon?*

"Brandon died last night."

Oh, no. Although expected, the news rocked Carrie. Every day the child clung to life, she hoped he would make it, in spite of the odds. "How sad," she managed to say. The trio walked to the hotel in silence.

After taking a shower, Carrie rummaged through her suitcase for a hairbrush. A ball of yarn rolled out. In the confusion of leaving Bucharest, Carrie had packed the partially crocheted baby sweater with her things.

The sleeve dangled from her hand, and Carrie began to cry. The same anger and helplessness she'd felt that day in the orphanage returned. No child should have to die.

At least Brandon knew his father's love. Not like those poor abandoned children.

"You could love them." A voice sounded inside her head.

Yes, but how?

"When you love them, you love Me."

God?

In her mind she saw Miron, the toddler who had AIDS, pleading with her. "Come back to Romania and help us."

five

"Father. Thank You for these men and women who have come to Romania to help spread the good news of Your salvation. May we work together for Your glory. Amen."

Once again Carrie sat in the warm quiet of St. Joseph's Church listening to Pastor Radu pray. *I'm really here. Back in Romania.* One year and college graduation later, she had returned. New faces with new names surrounded her. A smaller group than the Victory Singers, about twenty adults of all ages had committed to spending two years in Bucharest on short-term missions assignments.

"Mind if I sit here? I'm a little late." A vivacious blonde close to her own age took a seat next to Carrie. "Wow. My name's Michelle, by the way."

Mute, Carrie pointed to her name tag.

". . .will help Anika and me in starting new churches here in Bucharest. Campus ministry, Bible studies, whatever is your special area of interest and gifts. . ."

"Wonder what I'll be doing?"

If you listen, you might find out.

"A few of you have specialized interests, which we will discuss later. But for the next month you all must concentrate on learning the language. If you know any of the Romance languages, you will notice similarities."

Let's see. Good morning. Buna dimineata. *My few basic phrases won't get me very far. I know, I'll learn with the children!*

❧

"Are you sure you want to do this?" Anika asked as she drove through the city streets. "We would love to have you stay in Bucharest with us."

"Absolutely sure. God called me, and He'll get me through any rough spots." *I sound naive, but I believe it.*

Anticipation and apprehension built in equal measures as they turned onto a tree-lined drive and the stately old building came into view. Anika pounded the ancient door knocker and smiled her reassurance. Minutes passed, and the door swung open. At least a dozen elderly women crowded around Sister Pauline, matching smiles obliterating facial differences.

"Buna dimineata." The director stepped forward. "We've been looking forward to your arrival." Carrie rushed into her welcoming arms.

❧

"Congratulations, Coach. Great win. What do you think of the Broncos' chances this year?" A reporter was conducting a postgame interview.

Steve glanced up from the desk where he sat planning the marching band's next performance. *I missed the end of the game.* He smiled a rueful grin. Sports hadn't always marked the passage of time in his life. That had changed, like a lot of things, since—since Lila's death sixteen months ago.

Closing his eyes against the memories, he reviewed the band's marching patterns. *Get this one right, and we'll go to the state finals. What next?* The rake rested by the door, inviting him outside to tackle the golden aspen leaves that covered the lawn faster than he could take care of them.

Lila made a game of autumn leaves, jumping in tall piles like a child. Tears welled in his eyes. *Don't think about it.* He could imagine her standing by the door, rake in hand. *Not today,* she mouthed.

No, he had avoided the next task long enough. How often had Tim and Brenda offered to help him take down the nursery and find young families who could use the furniture and baby clothes? In his heart, Steve knew that the first time he turned the knob and opened the door to painful memories, he should go alone. He couldn't delay any longer. Today he was ready.

He flicked off the television set, turned his back on the inviting Indian summer afternoon, and walked toward the nursery. Lila had dubbed the hallway leading to the bedrooms the Romero Family Hall of Fame. How his fingers had trembled when he hung the picture of last year's Victory Singers, taken before they left New York. Lila's smile from the back row seemed meant for him alone, a shared joke, as if her fingers itched to make rabbit's ears. A snapshot of Lila crocheting something was stuck in one corner. Carrie had sent the picture along with a sympathy card. Nice kid. Kind to Lila at the end.

Dust obscured the glass now. Frowning, he located the paper towel and rubbed Lila's wedding portrait clear, restoring her white satin gown to shining brightness. The picture of his parents' twenty-fifth wedding anniversary anchored the other family pictures—Tim and Brenda, graduation, Sammy from infant to schoolboy, baby Amanda.

He dabbed at a few more spots and started straightening the frames. *I'm avoiding the nursery,* he realized. *It's got to be now.* Turning his back to the wall, he pushed the doorknob.

A musty smell tickled his nose, and he sneezed. He grabbed a tissue from a full box, where Lila had placed it so many months ago. Everything was the way he remembered it. Jungle animals danced around pale yellow walls. The crib, changing table, dresser, and rocking chair echoed empty loneliness.

On top of the dresser a stack of thank-you notes waited, ready to thank people for the gifts that lined the drawers. He tugged at the top handle. Dozens of sheets and baby blankets blinked at him with pastel colors. Sleepers in neutral shades of yellow and green filled the next drawer, with a few boyish suits and frilly dresses mixed in. The clothes were destined for a pregnancy center his church supported. He reached into the drawer then withdrew his hands. *How can I tear apart the nest we built? I need Tim and Brenda's help.*

He stumbled backwards into the rocking chair. A half-finished baby afghan draped across the wicker back, white, pink, and blue weaving in unpredictable patterns. A crochet hook protruded from a ball of yarn, waiting for Lila to return. He buried his face in the soft yarn. Tears came, gentle cries as if she joined him in mourning their son. Images of Lila and Brandon lived on his heart, undimmed by the passage of time.

The sky had turned dark when the sobs stopped, and he turned tear-stained eyes around the room. There was no reason to keep the nursery as a monument to love lost. His family stayed alive where they always would, in his memory. He crossed to the windows and opened them an inch. A draft of fresh autumn air flowed through the room, sweeping out the musty past with it.

❧

A week later, the front doorbell rang. A towel-covered casserole steamed in his sister Brenda's hands. Amanda, six months old at the time of the ill-fated trip to Romania, snuggled in Tim's arms.

"How you doing, Uncle Steve?" Sammy barged in, ran to the piano, and plunked out the first few notes of "Chopsticks."

"I'm fine, partner." Steve cocked his head, listening to his nephew play. "I think you're ready to start lessons."

"Really?" He hustled after his mother into the kitchen. "Can I, Mom?" Their soft voices carried whispers into the living room.

"Reporting for duty as promised." Tim glanced down the hall and pointed at the open door. "I see you've been in."

"Yeah." Steve took a deep breath, exhaled. "Last weekend."

When Steve didn't say anything else, Tim raised his eyebrows in silent questioning.

"I've put the casserole in the oven to keep warm." Brenda and Sammy reappeared from the kitchen. "Are you ready to get started?"

Something clicked inside Steve, as if a suit of iron armor meshed into place protecting his vulnerable inner self. He managed a half smile. "Sure. That's the plan." Before his resolve failed, he forged his way down the hall.

Sammy raced ahead of him then came to an abrupt standstill in the doorway, almost causing Steve to trip. "This was your baby's room," he said in a matter-of-fact voice. "The one who died."

Brenda halted beside Steve, eyes expressing distress over Sammy's thoughtless words.

"It's okay." Steve spoke to his sister over Sammy's head then tapped him on the shoulder. "Move out of the way, partner. You're blocking the entrance."

Amanda tottered into the room behind her brother and made a beeline for a soft brown teddy bear, the duplicate of one in her own nursery. Twisting a knob in the back, she laid her head against the chest that throbbed with the sound of a mother's heartbeat like a baby hears in the womb. The stuffed animal represented Steve and Lila's two-week search through baby stores and specialty catalogs.

"Wow! I love this!" The wall panel with its brightly colored jungle animals attracted Sammy. He hunched over and lumbered across the floor, clasping his hands where they dangled from his chest. "Guess what I am!"

"An elephant?" Tim answered from the doorway.

"Yes!" Sammy slid down on all fours and started growling. Steve couldn't drag his eyes away from the pretend lion. That could have been, should have been, Brandon.

Brenda gave him a side hug and looked into his eyes. They stood with arms intertwined for a brief moment.

"Thanks for coming, Sis."

"No problem. Where are the boxes?" She opened a drawer and began arranging sheets and blankets. "Sammy, give me a hand."

He tossed in a few toys before wandering out of the room. A minute later "Chopsticks" erupted in their ears.

Amanda looked into the rapidly filling container. Her arm dangled the teddy bear over the top. "Dark." She clutched the toy against her chest.

"Put the teddy bear in the box, Amanda."

"Later." Seeing the stuffed animal in Amanda's chubby arms connected the past to the present in Steve's mind. How could he give everything away? Pretend as if Brandon had never existed?

"Steve. Give me a hand here, will you?" Tim's voice floated through the air. Metal scraped against metal, and a bolt clanked to the floor. The crib tilted precariously as Tim unscrewed a second bolt with his right hand while holding another leg to the floor with his left. Glasses perched on the end of his long nose. The tool slipped and knocked his fingers. "Ouch."

Still all thumbs, except at the piano. A laugh rose to Steve's lips until he shushed it, ashamed at finding humor in Tim's awkward attempts to help. What would Lila think of this endeavor? During her pregnancy, exasperated, she had chased both men out and assembled the crib herself.

Once again Amanda tucked the teddy bear in the box and snatched it back. Music from the piano had switched to "Twinkle, Twinkle Little Star."

Steve looked around the room. Brenda had already emptied two drawers. A futon with plaid cushions waited in an opened box, ready to assemble and replace the partially dismantled crib. A sense of wrong washed over Steve. This room was perfect for a child. *I can't change it to a guest room. Not yet.*

"Ouch!" Tim exclaimed once more. "Help me, Steve."

Stop. "Stop!" Three pairs of eyes swung to stare at him, and Steve realized he must have shouted. "No more tonight."

The screwdriver slipped from Tim's hand, and Brenda folded the flaps of the box before standing up straight. "Well,

I guess it is time to check on supper," she said uncertainly and walked out the door. Tim looked at him over the top of his glasses, shrugged, and left.

Mixed feelings whirled around Steve's heart as the room emptied. Amanda tugged at his hand. He looked down into her trusting eyes. *How can I explain to her parents?*

Over bubbly macaroni and cheese, he tried. "I'd like to use the room the way it is." He struggled to explain his sudden reluctance to follow through on dismantling the nursery. "Like when Sammy or Amanda comes to visit." He forked a mouthful of casserole into his mouth and chewed for a minute. "Or even having a child live here."

"A foster child," Brenda said, spooning out more macaroni. "I bet you'd make a good foster parent, with your experience with kids."

"Or even—adoption." The word slipped out but surprised Steve when it felt comfortable and familiar.

"Adoption?" Brenda's voice sliced sharp with incredulity. Steve could almost hear her thoughts. *He's on the rebound. Trying to find what he's lost.*

"Don't worry, Sis. I'm not rushing into anything." He gulped down some milk. "Only, taking apart the nursery kind of feels like Abraham sacrificing Isaac, if you know what I mean. It's like God stayed my hand and stopped me from doing anything with the baby's things." He swallowed past the lump in his throat. *Not just a baby—Brandon!* "And I need to wait and see how God will provide."

"Hear, hear!" Tim struck a note with his fork and raised his hands like he was conducting a choir. "Let's toast the future!" As their glasses clinked together, he added, "And when you figure out what you want to do, we'll be there to help."

Adoption grew in Steve's mind, blossoming as quickly as a dandelion in spring and threatening to die as fast. When he contacted a local law firm, the attorney counseled against trying.

"There are few infants available for adoption. As for older children—most agencies prefer placing children with parents of the same race. That eliminates many of them as well." The sad frown the lawyer assumed melted into an almost-greedy smile when he added, "Unless you know a birth mother who wants to give up her child. . . ?" When Steve shook his head in the negative, the lawyer handed him a schedule of expected costs for private adoption. Steve tried to hide his shock. *The fees shouldn't surprise me, but they do.*

He tried Social Services next. Some foster parents he knew had adopted children they had raised since birth. It was early November before a caseworker could arrange for a home evaluation.

Late one afternoon a middle-aged woman with straight, streaked-blond hair knocked on his door. "Hello, I'm Susan Stewart from Denver Social Services. I believe you're expecting me?"

He invited her in. Probing blue eyes swept over him, as if assessing his fitness for parenthood. Steve repressed a defensive reaction. *I want to get on her good side.*

She padded in soft-soled shoes through the house. In the living room she dived for the electrical outlets. "You will child-proof, of course. Cover unused outlets." Steve nodded, thinking of the way Tim and Brenda had combed their house for danger points.

In the kitchen she turned on a burner. "Gas stove, I see."

I'll get electric if it's safer.

She turned on the faucets in the bathroom and poked her head in linen closets and Steve's bedroom before entering the nursery. For the first time a hint of a smile lightened her serious face. "What a lovely room for a baby."

A compliment. Steve's heartbeat began to accelerate before she continued.

"But many children who need foster care are older, already in school. Most have a history of abuse and neglect and subsequent behavior problems."

"I know. Some of my band students live in foster homes." The words came out before Steve could bite back the defensive reaction.

"Ah, yes. I remember." The assessing tone of her voice unnerved Steve. "You're a high school music teacher." She flicked off the light switch. "I've seen all I need to. Let's go out to the living room. To talk."

"Can I get you something to drink?" Steve hunted for something to postpone the upcoming interview. "I can brew some coffee. Or would you prefer tea?"

"Nothing for me. Thank you." She sat down on the couch and snapped open a briefcase. "Mr. Romero. Relax. I promise I won't bite."

Her well-controlled voice might defuse tense situations, but it set Steve's teeth on edge. He poured himself a glass of tea, took a sip, and licked his lips. Settling in an easy chair, he motioned for the caseworker to begin. "Okay. Let's get started."

The questioning probed everything and overlooked nothing. The detailed financial worksheet made Steve wonder how he expected to support himself in retirement, let alone provide for someone else. Who would care for a child while he worked? How long had he been teaching? What about band trips?

Although expected, the questions regarding marriage disturbed Steve. *She knows my wife is dead.* Nowadays, the marital status box for "widowed" leaped off any application. *Why make me explain?*

"What about marriage? Family?" She repeated.

"My wife died while we were in Romania last year."

"And the nursery?" she persisted.

Steve borrowed her detached manner for a patient answer. "Lila was pregnant at the time. She died giving birth to our son, and he died ten days later."

She looked up from her notes. "I'm sorry." She wrote a few

more words. "I must ask you. Are you involved in any serious relationships at present?"

He shook his head mutely.

The questions continued. What experience did he have with children? What methods of discipline did he advocate? What about religion?

She scribbled some final notes and locked her briefcase with a snap. "That's all for now. The department will be in touch."

"When?" Worry and longing filled his voice. Steve's efforts at mirroring her disinterested manner failed him in the end.

"In a few weeks." When they parted at the door, Steve couldn't read any indication either way.

Early in December, the phone rang. "Mr. Romero, this is Susan Stewart. The caseworker from Social Services."

"Yes?" Steve's mouth went dry.

"I wanted to tell you myself." Her voice held more warmth than she had demonstrated during the entire interview.

Steve steeled himself. *Either way, God is in control.*

"Your application was given serious consideration, but in the end it was turned down."

A coldness stole into Steve's heart. "What was the problem? Is there anything I can do?"

"I'm afraid not." After a brief silence, she continued. "I probably shouldn't be telling you this. You would be an excellent candidate if you were married. Or if you weren't so involved with your church."

Knowing he was fighting a rearguard action, Steve protested weakly. "But there are single foster parents."

"Yes."

"So the big problem is church?"

"Try to understand. The rights of birth parents come first, and the department has had problems when foster parents have a strong faith." Again her voice offered warmth. "Imagine if you can that a family of practicing Muslims was caring for your child."

Steve mumbled something, he wasn't sure what. What did one say when one's hopes were disappointed—again? Some of his friends would call this religious persecution.

"Mr. Romero. . ." He tuned out her attempt to end a difficult phone call until he heard ". . .foreign adoption?"

"What's that?" *I sound lame.* "I'm sorry. What did you say?"

"I asked if you have considered foreign adoption. The requirements may be less strict."

Foreign? As in Korean? Romanian? "No, I haven't. But I might be interested." *Are you crazy, Steve?*

"I'll send you a list of agencies that specialize in overseas adoption, if you like."

"Yes. Please."

"I'll put it in the mail tomorrow, then. God bless." The phone clicked in Steve's ear.

Not uncaring—just professional, Steve realized.

Romania? Maybe. Romania? Yes! God had opened the next door for him to explore.

❧

About a week before Christmas, Steve answered a ringing phone.

"You might want to sit down, Mr. Romero." Somehow the smile transmitted over telephone wires. Excitement built in Steve's heart and tingled to his fingertips, where the earphone trembled in his hand. He stood frozen in place, waiting for the announcement.

"Do you have a current passport?"

Passport? Romania! Sweat poured down his arms, and the phone slipped in his hand.

"Ah, yes. Does this mean—?"

"Congratulations! Your application has been approved! How soon can you fly to Bucharest?"

six

So many women clustered around Carrie, introducing themselves, that she quickly gave up hope of remembering their names. One by one they returned to their duties, leaving her with the director and Cristina, the woman with Down's syndrome.

Carrie followed them inside. The door closed, shutting out sunshine and ties with America. The place loomed larger and gloomier than she remembered. *I thought it would be like my college dorm. But it's not.*

"I'm glad you're here." Sister Pauline added her welcome while she paused at the door to her office. "Cristina will take you to your room. After you've settled in, meet me here so that we can discuss your future."

Smiling widely, Cristina escorted Carrie to the end of the hall and opened the door. "Here is your room. I helped get it ready for you."

Sunshine slanted through transparent curtains, bouncing off a gleaming wooden floor. Simple cotton covers adorned the thin mattress. She was pleased to see a sink in the corner. Suddenly she felt grimy all over and hoped to freshen up before her visit with Sister Pauline.

"Thanks. It's lovely." Carrie spoke in what she hoped was a tone of dismissal to the lingering Cristina.

"Can I help you unpack?"

Carrie shook her head in the negative.

"I will wait and bring you back to Sister."

"No, really, I'm fine." Desperate for a moment alone in her new surroundings, Carrie spoke more sharply than she intended. Cristina's smile faltered.

Impatient already. "Thanks for all your help. Maybe I'll see you at supper?"

"*Jah,* that would be good." Smile restored, Cristina left the room, shutting the door gently behind her.

Carrie walked to the sink and turned on the tap. Cupping her hands under the lukewarm water, she splashed water on her hot neck. Unpacking took only a few minutes. It was time to brave the lion's den. After she said a brief prayer, she strode down the hallway and knocked on the office door.

"Please come in. Sit down."

Awkwardness as strong as her first day at freshman initiation came over Carrie. *What if she doesn't like me?* She sat down on the chair, slamming her knees together to keep them from knocking.

"Carrie Randolph from Pennsylvania. How wonderful that God has brought you here."

All of Carrie's doubts dropped away as she looked into Sister Pauline's peaceful, hopeful eyes. The director outlined the schedule for the next few days.

"We keep to a routine here, and we will expect you to do the same. We meet for prayer at 6:30 a.m. and 10:00 at night, except for the sisters on duty on the wards. Meals at 7:30, 12:00, and 7:00. Cristina does the staff laundry each Monday—leave your clothes in the hallway."

Carrie nodded her head impatiently. "Okay. Where will I be working?"

The sister smiled faintly. "I think it would be best for you to choose a small group of children—four, five at most—to work with."

"No." Carrie wasn't sure if she actually said the word. She rebelled at the thought. "I thought I might be spelling the ward sisters, you know, working with all the children."

Pauline bowed her head as if in prayer then dipped her chin

in a gentle assent. "Very well. We will set up a rotation system for you to work this week. Next Monday we will see how things are going."

A few days later, Carrie didn't hear any alarm until the chapel bell pealed, calling her to morning prayers. Her muscles cramped in pain as she scrambled out of bed and into a short-sleeved shirt and jeans. The top went on the wrong way, and she wasted precious moments shifting it around. She flew down the stairs to the chapel and slipped into the back pew.

Upon her arrival, an almost audible sigh of relief rippled across the room. At times like this she felt a bit like Maria von Trapp, perpetually late, a likable troublemaker. The sisters welcomed her with open arms but didn't quite know what to do with her.

She wanted to fit in, to give aid, not require it. God knew she had tried. For five days she had run from ward to ward, ferrying bottles and laundry, changing diapers, walking with two or three howling babies, names unknown, in her arms. Every muscle ached with fatigue.

As she scurried about, she caught the director watching her at times. It made her uneasy, like when her music teachers coaxed and listened, waiting for something to happen. Finally the melody would sing out loud and clear, and they would smile in satisfaction. If only she knew what Sister Pauline was looking for!

On Monday she met with the director for a second time. They went back through each ward on every floor in all five buildings. Sister Pauline stopped periodically to prop up a milk bottle or to tug a blanket over a sleeping form. When they reached the end of the row, one child howled, starting a chain reaction in which all two dozen infants cried.

The sound caught Carrie as effectively as a trap, immobilizing her in place.

"Let's go. Leave the sister to take care of them." Pauline touched her arm and led her through the door. Outside the soundproof walls, away from the mesmerizing noise, Carrie broke out of her trance, and unbidden tears cascaded down her face.

"They're so demanding! And I feel so inadequate." Carrie wanted to storm back into the nursery and gather every crying child into her arms.

"Come with me to the chapel." Sister Pauline gently steered the weeping Carrie away from the wards.

They sat side by side in the pew. Clasping Carrie's trembling hands between her own gnarled fingers, Sister Pauline reminded her, "When our Lord was here on this earth, He chose to pour His life into twelve men only—and they were adults! You would be wise to follow His example." *That's what she meant*—

"Children require individual attention in order to thrive. You are only one person. Choose a small group of four or five. Ask God to show you which ones."

Carrie slowly nodded in understanding and agreement. "But how can I choose? They're all so needy!"

"Pray," Pauline reminded her. "Our Lord spent the night in prayer before He chose the twelve apostles. He will show you."

Prayer again. How about something practical?

"You seem impatient with the time we spend in prayer."

She knows me already. Carrie thought guiltily of all her late arrivals at the required chapel hours.

"We find that the busier we are, the more we need to pray. The chapel is always open, for any time you need to seek God's face." She gestured for Carrie to join her at the kneeling bench. "You will find your answers, and strength, here."

For the next week Carrie haunted the wards by day and knelt for hours at night. After seven days, she had decided. All five slept in the toddler ward in the building that she visited on her trip a year ago: sweet Jenica, cranky Octavia, active Adrian, puttering Ion. And first of all, dearest of all,

Viktor, who sang himself to sleep in his crib.

❧

Her breath formed warm rings that floated through the frosty air as she walked to the toddler ward. It was time to begin the morning-long effort of going to market.

At the top of the stairs, Sister Marie waited, chin nodding against her chest. She willingly took the night shift, love enabling her to climb up and down the steep stairs.

Carrie pressed her foot against the top step. It squeaked as she expected, and Marie lifted up her head in greeting.

"Good morning!" Carrie started sorting the clothes that lay in a jumbled heap on the floor of the communal closet. Marie unbent her body with care and fumbled through the key ring with her bent fingers.

"How are the children?" Carrie located enough shirts, pants, and socks for everyone, and even an extra sweater for Ion. Shoes and coats were another matter.

"Ion's cough is a little worse, I'm afraid. Praise God, no fever."

Oh, Lord, please, make him well! She extracted the key from Marie's hand and, drawing a deep breath, unlocked the door.

Finding herself the mother of quintuplets at age twenty-two challenged Carrie to the limit. They were her constant companions. She fed, bathed, and dressed them, and somehow found time to play with them. Most of all they needed to be around people.

Dozens of voices cried, "Mama." Steeling her nerves, Carrie hustled through the room to where Jenica waited, silently watching. When Carrie neared her crib, the girl lifted her arms expectantly. Carrie's heart twisted. *This is why I'm here. So they can learn to love, to trust.* Moments like this made up for the long hours.

A few beds further on Adrian tugged furiously at his sock. *Always taking it on or off.* Not many of the children made an effort at dressing themselves.

A frowning Octavia waited in her usual spot in the middle of her crib, as if daring Carrie to reach her. Smothering a sigh, she called a cheerful greeting. "Good morning, Octavia." Stretching, Carrie latched on to the child with arms of steel. *Ion next.*

She could pick out Ion's cough from that of the other chronically sick children. *Marie is right; it's worse than last night.* It was discouraging. He needed medical care, but Dr. Reynaud wouldn't return for six more weeks. Hot compresses and tea with lemon and honey only did so much good. Why use the home's limited supplies when he wasn't getting better? A warm, dry room to sleep in would probably make a big difference. He spent most nights soaking wet. Carrie powdered his bare bottom and pinned a stiff new diaper in place. No disposable diapers here!

Carrie could always locate Viktor by his humming—snatches of Romanian folk songs, church music, tunes he made up himself. "Where is Viktor? Where is Viktor? Here he is!" She sang to the tune of "Frère Jacques" as she approached his crib. Soon he joined the others on the floor next to her.

After breakfast they were ready to go to market. The trip, easy by bicycle, involved an unpleasant trek over frozen mud by foot. Although Carrie used the bike in emergencies, most of the time she walked so that the children could go with her. She wanted them to have as much stimulation as possible—fresh air, new sounds, sights, colors. Besides, she enjoyed their company.

They padded silently alongside her, rarely speaking, even though child development charts said children their age should have a fairly extensive vocabulary. Not for the first time she wondered, *Do they even know how to speak?* Along the road she looked for things they might recognize and chattered the way she did with babies.

"Look! There's a sparrow! The tree has lost its leaves. It looks so sad. The squirrel must be looking for the nuts he hid away last fall."

"Cat," Jenica called out.

Yes! A scrawny tiger cat sat on a fence post watching their progress. "Here, kitty, kitty." The animal looked warily at the children then allowed Carrie to pick it up. Curling up in Carrie's hands, it licked her fingers and began purring with a loud, contented sound.

Carrie held Jenica's fingers to the kitten's throat so that she could feel the vibrating purr that shook the small body.

"Me next!" Not satisfied with fingers only, Viktor laid his ear next to the cat's neck and tried to mimic the sound. A small scuffle ensued as each child wanted a chance to pet the kitten. *Yes!* Carrie breathed a short prayer of thanksgiving. God had given them something that broke through their unnerving silence.

The sun began edging its way to the zenith of the sky, and reluctantly Carrie headed toward the market. *We'll be late for lunch if we don't get moving.*

First they stopped at the vegetable vendor's stand. "Feel this one. It's a good, firm one." Carrie picked through the potatoes, letting the children push and prod the spuds with her.

"Why don't you leave those stupid children at the orphanage? Then you and me, we could have some fun." The vendor, a heavy man she had heard was a widower with seven children, teased her.

"They aren't stupid!" Of all the customs that were different than ones in the States, calling children stupid because they had been abandoned bothered her the most.

"I know. They are the future!" He pointed at Viktor. "This one here you think will be a great musician!" Gesturing at Adrian, he said, "And this one, he will compete in the Olympic games! Pah!" He spat. "I still say they're stupid."

Forcing herself to ignore his jibes, she handed over the correct number of *lei,* the Romanian currency, and went to the next booth. With five children trailing behind her, she felt a bit like the Pied Piper, leading them with her songs and storytelling.

What I wouldn't give for a supermarket. Never again would she complain about lines. An hour passed, and each child carried a light bag as they trudged back to the orphanage for the noon meal.

After lunch—an hour and a half marathon that ended with folding clean sheets on Ion's bed and tucking each child in for a nap—Carrie headed to her room. During her afternoon free time, she hoped to finish one mitten, maybe a pair. Cold weather was a powerful motivator to practice crocheting! *I'm forgetting something.* She considered briefly but couldn't place the worry. Under her fingers, a bright yellow mitten cuff began to grow. Funny how Lila had sparked her interest in the craft. *I wonder how Steve is doing these days?*

"Carrie?" Sister Pauline called at her door.

"Come in." As Carrie stood up, a ball of yarn rolled out of her lap onto the floor. She stuffed it under her unmade bed covers.

The director ignored the bed and addressed Carrie. "I wondered if you wanted to come with me to say good-bye to Irina."

How could I forget? Irina was the blonde toddler with crossed eyes that Carrie met on her first trip to the home.

"Of course." In short order Carrie shrugged on her downy ski jacket, hat, and mittens, and followed Sister Pauline down the hallway.

The sisters often asked Carrie to escort visiting Americans and Britons around the wards, a duty she usually enjoyed. Today was different, though. David and Donna Johnson were taking little Irina to their home in Cleveland, Ohio. The last papers had been signed and permission granted for them to take their new daughter home.

I won't see Irina anymore. The thought stabbed into Carrie, and she crossed her arms across her chest as if to keep out the impending loss.

"This day may come for one of your children, as well. I pray that it does." Sister Pauline, sensitive as always, somehow knew what Carrie was thinking.

"That would be wonderful for the children! Especially poor Ion." She meant it. Of course she did.

"I am praying for you that when that day comes, our Lord will give you grace to let them go." Sister Pauline laid a hand on Carrie's arm and halted their progress for a minute. "Loving comes with a price. It cost our Lord His life. But even though it will be painful to see your beloved children leave, He will see you through."

They exited the building. Donna held Irina in her arms. The couple's overabundant happiness more than made up for the child's bewildered silence. David kissed the top of her head. "Soon you'll be home with us. Your new grandparents can't wait to meet you." He spoke in English. *How will Irina manage? She barely speaks Romanian.*

Unexpected tears slid down Carrie's cheeks. "God bless you, Irina," she said in Romanian and kissed the girl's cool cheek. "Take good care of her, won't you?" she added in English.

David smiled his agreement, overjoyed and confident about what he was doing. Feeling her own heart wrench, Carrie better understood the parents who wouldn't agree to adoption, even though they knew it might be best for their child.

Soon Donna buckled Irina in a back car seat where she squirmed against the uncomfortable restraint. David dug through the bag with her few personal items, removed her security blanket, a worn scarf, and returned the rest to Sister Pauline. "Keep them. Perhaps other children can use them."

They waved good-bye as the car spun out of the yard. The sisters returned to their tasks, and for the moment Carrie stood alone in the yard.

"Good-bye, Irina," The words seemed to hang in the air, frozen, and then float away with the departing car. She walked briskly back to the dorm. Thank goodness tomorrow was her free day. A good dose of big-city comforts and American companionship should cure her blues.

❧

"There's an American staying with Radu and Anika." From the tone of Michelle's voice, her romantic antennae were quivering.

"Oh? Tell me about him." Carrie stirred her coffee, basking in the deliciously warm American superstore in downtown Bucharest.

"He's so good-looking, with a touch of melancholy. Makes you want to cheer him up." Michelle's eyes blinked in surprise. "I didn't tell you their guest was a man!"

"I guessed right, though, didn't I?" Carrie grinned. During language study the previous summer, she and Michelle fell into an easy friendship. Immersed most of the time in a foreign culture, they welcomed the opportunity to meet together once a week and act like giddy American ingenues. Michelle was an incurable romantic, weaving fantasies about every man who caught her eye.

"What happened to that taxi driver? Anka, wasn't that his name?" Carrie asked.

"Oh, him." Michelle's cheeks dimpled. "It turns out he's engaged. He invited me to his wedding! How about you? Have you met anyone?" Michelle was a determined matchmaker.

"Well, there's Paul the potato vendor—"

"Oh?"

"He's single, and he has lovely wavy hair—"

"Why haven't you told me about him before?"

"—that's snow white. He must be at least sixty years old, with two dozen grandchildren!"

Michelle tossed a lettuce leaf on Carrie's plate.

"Seriously, how could I meet a single man at a Romanian orphanage?"

"It could happen. You do get visitors at the home, like that

Dr. Reynaud you rave about. Is he single?"

A clock chimed in the distance before Carrie could voice her indignant reply. "Goodness, it's late. I suppose we should get started with the Christmas shopping." Michelle scraped her fork over the plate one more time, seeking out the last pastry crumb.

"I sent presents home a month ago," Carrie said as she perused her list. "Today I'm looking for gifts for my group. Dolls, soccer balls. Those should be easy. But where can I find a child's tool set? Or a recorder?"

"Tape recorder? Don't you think that's kind of extravagant?"

"No, a recorder. You know, the flute-thing children play in school as a first instrument. For—"

"Viktor. Your favorite." Before Carrie could deny the observation, Michelle swept on. "I know just the place to look."

Carrie folded the paper and tucked it back in her purse. "It's funny. I bought Romanian-made items for my family in Pennsylvania. Now all I can think of for the children are things I enjoyed as a child in America!" She drained her coffee cup. "Let's go."

It's such a very American store. Carrie sighed with pleasure. A fifteen-foot tall tree, adorned with red, blue, and yellow balls and metallic garlands, towered over the escalators. Miniature lights alternated with neon Santas on wires strung between every pillar and along every counter.

Rolls of colorful foil beckoned to Carrie. She pulled out three long packages, one each of blue, gold, and green.

"Red for me." Michelle made her selection.

"I can't wait to see the children rip their presents open." Carrie's forehead wrinkled. "Does this stuff tear easily? I don't remember." Glancing around furtively, she yanked at the edge of one roll. A piece came off in her hand. The friends smiled at each other with a hint of mischievous guilt.

Carrie shopped for the girls first. Even after excluding

English-speaking dolls and ones that needed batteries, there were so many to choose from. She settled on a doll that changed facial expressions for Octavia and a simple baby with bottle for Jenica.

The store stocked a wide variety of soccer equipment, with a smattering of other sports. Carrie ignored the ads that announced, "The ball that won the World Cup!" and poked through the children's balls. Did a lower number mean it was bigger or smaller? She found one in the smallest size for Adrian.

"Why not a football?" Michelle suggested.

"It *is* a football. European football." Carrie stated the obvious. "Adrian is a Romanian, after all. Soccer gives him a way to connect with other kids." She paid for her purchases and stuffed them in a voluminous shopping bag. "Where did you think I could find a recorder?"

"A store about two blocks from here carries them." They walked down the street. "Why are you spending so much on toys?" Michelle asked abruptly. "With all their other needs—"

"Mom's missions society took on the entire ward as a Christmas project. You've never seen so many afghans and quilts and coats and sweaters. Knitting needles working overtime. So the practical presents were taken care of." Looking down at the packages in her hand, she said, "I guess I always go overboard for Christmas. Only I want the children to have some fun. I bet they've never had any toys."

"Poor kids!" Michelle's admiration was genuine. "I don't think I could stand working in the home."

"And I couldn't do what you do. Knocking on doors and waiting for people to show up at a Bible study." Carrie hugged her friend.

By the time they had purchased the remaining presents, a church clock was chiming four o'clock, time to catch the bus back to the home. A few minutes later, the vehicle jerked to a stop on the street, and Carrie climbed aboard. "See you next week!" she called through the closing doors.

❧

"You will like the director," Anika told Steve as they headed for the orphanage. "She is a sweet saint of God."

"But all is not sweetness at the children's home," Radu interjected. "I hear the American news has reported on our orphans?" The statement ended like a question.

Steve nodded his assent. "The situation sounded grim." He didn't elaborate.

"The situation is sad. But God is at work." A peaceful smile lit Radu's face. "He has used those reports to bring many foreigners to our country to adopt the children. Good from evil. Like your own tragedy." He never minced words.

The sting of the words couldn't penetrate Steve's excitement. "I can't wait. Ever since the idea of adoption occurred to me, I've been hungry for a child to call my own. After what happened here—" Momentarily his voice faltered. "Romania was one of the first places I thought of."

"And this afternoon you may find your answer. Here we are."

A few minutes later they were settled in the office. Introductions made, Steve shifted in his chair while an elderly woman studied his papers. "Your wife died?" Radu translated.

"Yes." Her eyes continued to question him, and he didn't mind elaborating. "She died giving birth to our son. He died a few days later." How could he explain his desire to adopt? "When the grief had passed, I realized I still wanted to be a father."

"You are a good man, Mr. Romero. Perhaps God has the child you seek here." Her smile radiated from the inside out.

Someone knocked at the door.

"Here is the person who will take you through the wards."

Crying baby in arms, Lila's image appeared, flickered, and reshaped into her look-alike.

"Carrie! What on earth are you doing here?"

seven

"Steve?" Carrie's dumbfounded expression probably matched his own. "You're the American Michelle was telling me about!"

Why didn't Radu warn me?

Sister Pauline appeared to be asking for explanations. Radu spread his hands and gestured to the two young people. An expression full of understanding, then compassion, crossed the director's face.

"I'm on a short-term volunteer assignment," Carrie explained. "I've been here since I graduated from college in June." She shifted the child to her other arm. "And you? How have you been? Are you really thinking about adopting?"

Steve couldn't look at Carrie without remembering the night at the hospital. He swallowed back the tears that threatened and found his voice. "Yeah, I am. I understand you're going to show me around."

"Sure."

Any further dialogue was cut off by the arrival of one of the staff, a middle-aged woman with a placid face. Carrie handed over the now-sleeping child with apparent reluctance and motioned for Steve to follow her.

"Is he all right? The kid you were holding?" *Focus on the present. Don't talk about the past.*

"Ion? He has a terrible cold, can't sleep for coughing. They don't like me to walk with him, though. I guess I'm a softie." She folded her face in a self-deprecating grin. "Are you interested in any particular age group? The toddlers are taking their afternoon naps—"

"How about babies, then?"

Carrie nodded and led him to the second building. "Have you been to any other children's homes?"

Steve shook his head. "Radu and Anika brought me here first, since they know Sister Pauline."

"It's pretty grim." She paused at the door.

"I've heard." Suddenly the surroundings dropped away. His future lay in one of these buildings, and he was impatient with further delay. Hand on knob, he swung the door wide open.

The atmosphere of the room hit him like fog. The stench of urine, strong enough to bleach an army of uniforms, caused him to retch, a brief dry heave. Babies' cries born of discomfort, hunger, and loneliness streaked through the air, with no one seeming to hear or respond. His breath blew rings in the air, and he became aware of the coldness seeping up his coat sleeves. Carrie came in behind him and closed the door.

A thin woman walked toward them, exhaustion and disinterest showing in every step. Steam rose from a stinking bucket she held by one hand. Carrie called out a greeting. The woman waved thanks as she veered away toward the bathroom.

"Ready?" Carrie was already moving in the direction of the cribs, as if she didn't notice the assault on the senses.

C'mon, Steve, you're not going to let a little stink get you down! Okay, a big stink. Mentally pinching his nose, Steve followed along.

Carrie knew each child's name and often added a piece of personal information. "John—just arrived here a month ago." She tweaked a blanket over the sleeping form. "Ana's been here since she was born, but her mother won't give permission for adoption." Some of the babies were even tinier than he remembered Brandon to be. How did they survive? Did he want to adopt a child with obvious physical problems?

At his side, Carrie paused occasionally, as if waiting for him to express interest, ask questions. He noticed she was wearing only a thin sweater, and he shivered on her behalf. He started to offer her his coat then checked himself. The cold didn't seem to bother her. But what about the children? Coughing and sneezing punctuated the raucous cries.

The constant noise and oppressive odor combined the worst aspects of nursery duty at church. *Maybe I'm not cut out for this. At least not with a baby.* He found himself hurrying past the cribs, not really paying attention to Carrie. Doubts wrinkled his heart.

An hour later—or was it two?—they walked out into the sunshine. Steve gulped down the fresh air, not minding the cold burning his throat. *God, why did you bring me here?* He felt much like Samuel when he visited in Jesse's home. Is this the one? Not yet.

A strangely familiar, featherlight touch landed on his arm. It felt natural. "Are you all right?"

He breathed deeply. "I think so." *Exhale breath on a slow ten count.* "How do you stand it?"

"You get used to it." He noticed that she had pulled on a jacket. "You have to. What next? There's another nursery in the next building."

"No!" The word exploded out of his mouth. "Are the toddlers awake yet?"

"Sure." They walked past the stark high-rise.

"Back there, you were wondering how the children survive."

How did she know?

"A lot of them do die." Tears underlined her words. "But Sister Pauline says the question isn't why do so many die? Instead, we should ask, how do so many live? And thank God." Compassionate pain filled her grimace. "I try to hold on to that."

The last building came into view, and her walk speeded into

a skip. "The toddlers. My favorites." A genuine, full-hearted grin lit her face this time. She flung open the door and scampered up a flight of stairs before he had taken the first step.

"Buna dimineata!" a quavery voice welcomed Carrie in a way that indicated a close friendship.

"Come on," Carrie urged him. "Most of them are awake." To judge by her enthusiasm, this room should be as cheerful as his home church's nursery. To him it looked just as dreary, if not quite as smelly, as the infants' room.

"Mama!" several voices called out, and Carrie darted around the room, lifting out first one child then another. Soon four children, two boys and two girls, crowded around her feet, and the same boy she had sent to bed earlier curled against her shoulder.

Carrie bounced back to Steve, children dragging at her heels. "Hope you don't mind the gang. They go wherever I go." She must have sensed his bewilderment.

"This is my group. Let me introduce you." She rattled off a string of Romanian words, of which he only recognized his name.

"You've already met Ion." The child stared dumbly at Steve, thumb stuck in his mouth. "And this is Jenica. Octavia. Adrian." She caressed each one on the head as she introduced them.

"And Viktor." Was it just his imagination, or did her voice have an extra lift?

The children clustered around Carrie, pushing each other for a chance to hold on to her jean leg. They reminded Steve of Amanda and Sammy vying for his attention, and he relaxed. They were only children, after all, and hopefully God would show him which one soon.

A low musical humming played with Steve's ears, a familiar Victory Singers number. It didn't sound like Carrie. "Who's singing?"

"Oh!" Her smile had all the pride of the parents of his band students. "That's Viktor. He loves music."

The singing stopped at Steve's glance, and something tugged at his heart. He crouched down and rocked on his heels so he could look the boy in the eye.

"That's one of my favorite songs, too." Steve hummed through the introduction, the intricate chords echoing in his head, and started singing the first verse. Viktor's eyes widened as if in surprise, and his body swayed to the strong beat. Steve grasped his hands and clapped them together in time to the music when he reached the chorus.

"Sing it, Viktor!" Carrie's voice intruded. Legs dancing a jaunty two-step, she whirled around the man and child, and her voice rose high above Steve's bass, a spontaneous descant.

Viktor laughed, delighted, and shouted what was probably the one recognizable word in the song—victory!—and pointed to himself. "Viktor."

This is the one. Months of longing and searching faded, replaced by certainty and joy.

The music died away, and once again the dingy, cold room forced itself into Steve's consciousness. A dozen children stared curiously at their outburst.

"That was fun!" Carrie's eyes danced with lively merriment.

Steve smiled in return, a smile he couldn't contain. *I've found my son!* As suddenly as thunder follows lightning, his decision was made.

Ahead of him, Carrie circled around the back of the room, singing nursery rhymes with the children. *She's like their mother. If I adopt Viktor, will she be pleased—or sad?* The room darkened, and outside the windows, dusk staked its claim over daylight. The thought of causing Carrie sadness pained his heart. *Don't be too hasty.* "It's time for me to go," Steve said, regret tingeing his voice.

"But you've only met half the children." Nosy excitement written on her face, she asked, "Or do you already have someone in mind? Who—?" She paused in mid-sentence. "I'm sorry. It's none of my business. But you could do worse than to choose one of these angels."

"I've seen enough for today." He hedged. "It's five o'clock. Radu and Anika will be waiting for me."

Carrie escorted Steve downstairs, children trailing behind. "Can you find your way back from here? If you don't mind waiting, I'll take you." She gestured at the children. "Putting on coats is a half-hour process."

"That's all right." They stared at each other for a long moment, Steve once again sensing the shadows of Lila's beloved face in Carrie's features. Spending two years in a Romanian orphanage was the sort of thing Lila might have done. A nearly buried pang of grief hit his heart. He needed to leave, but he couldn't tear himself away.

"I'm glad you're doing this." The words blurted out of Carrie's mouth. "Lila told me you'd make a terrific father."

Lila. Her image hung between them, Carrie but a pale imitation. Would he ever look at another woman without comparing her to his wife? "Thanks."

"I guess this is it, then." Octavia made a small cry, and Carrie patted her head. "It's their supper time."

"I'll be back." He needed a day or two to weigh his decision to adopt Viktor. "After Christmas, maybe."

"I'd like that." She smiled and turned in the direction of the smell of greasy food cooking.

The outside door swung open. "Carrie!" Anika's warm voice echoed in the entryway. "I'm glad I found you."

Carrie paused. Her shoulders sagged a quarter of an inch, and Steve realized how tired she must be.

"I want you and the children to join us for Christmas."

Anika's oval face beamed, as if she were offering a priceless gift.

"But—it's not my day off. I'm needed here—"

"Sister Pauline agreed you could come."

"Well, then!" Carrie grinned. "I'd love to." Two of the children started to whimper. "I'm sorry, I must go. Bye for now!"

❧

Back at the small apartment, Steve and Anika shifted papers in an attempt to create a play space for the children. "I wish we could take them to the park. That would be perfect. But it's too cold," Anika fretted.

Steve shivered inside his thick sweater. The apartment wasn't warm, although compared to the children's home it felt like a desert.

Anika hummed to herself as she worked, cheerful songs that Steve guessed were Christmas carols. His suspicion was confirmed when he recognized the tune of "Silent Night," sung with unfamiliar words. He joined her, singing in English until the last note died away. What else might they both know? "O Come All Ye Faithful"? Soon they were singing an impromptu duet. Every tribe and tongue and nation—the words hit Steve afresh.

How could a baby born in a borrowed stable halfway around the globe be the Lord and Savior of the world? God's plans often didn't make sense. Like Lila's death?

Steve shook away the disquieting thought, only to have it followed by another idea. A red cord of love led from Lila and Brandon's death to the here and now—to Romania. To seeing Carrie again. To Viktor. The message of the incarnation—God came to the world to give beauty for ashes, the oil of gladness instead of mourning.

"Joy to the world!" Steve's voice rang out afresh, rejoicing in God's ultimate gift to the world—His only Son. Soon boxes were stacked and floor space cleared, awaiting their small guests on the following day.

That night Steve slept fitfully in the front sitting room. With the heat turned off for the night, cold permeated his bones and even the thick covers did not hold sufficient body warmth. What would Christmas in Romania be like? In all his previous trips overseas, he had always traveled in the summer. Back in Denver, it was still Christmas Eve. Tim and Brenda would be attending church with the children. *Next year,* he promised himself, *I'll go with them, my son or daughter by my side.*

He wrapped himself in blankets and sat by the front window, watching the day dawn. A light snow was falling, eiderdown soft and white with the promise of a new beginning.

Anika bustled into the room, lighting the fire. "Merry Christmas!" she called, kissing Steve on the cheek.

Radu blundered after her, caught her in a bear hug, and spoke, words muffled in her hair. "Christ is born!"

I don't belong here. Loneliness swamped Steve afresh. *I don't belong anywhere.* Half of a matching pair, he had lost part of his identity with Lila. *It's only the holidays. Things will seem brighter when they're over. It's not as bad as last year.* Maybe when Carrie and the children arrived, he wouldn't feel like the odd man out.

After breakfast—a feast of homemade sweet rolls, fresh fruit, and strong coffee—Anika drove to the home to pick up Carrie and the children. Steve walked with Radu to the church to turn on the heat for the service that would be held later that day. Anika's car chugged down the street when they returned to the apartment.

Steve nearly laughed. It looked so like a clown's car, every spare inch crammed. Four children perched on half of the back seat, surrounded by gaily decorated boxes. Carrie sat in the front, one of the boys leaning against her. They stopped, and

Anika stepped around to the passenger's side to let Carrie out.

Woman and child spilled out, with the rather awkward grace of a young colt. A Santa red coat wrapped around Carrie, a splash of cheer against the white snow. The children slowly climbing out of the car wore new coats that filled the street with warm yellows and greens and pinks.

Their matching expressionless faces stared at Steve. Only Viktor seemed to remember him, pointing his index finger and humming the chorus from "Victory in Jesus."

Yes! Steve's heart trembled with joy, and he sang the words, voice hoarse with emotion. "Merry Christmas," he whispered, as much to himself as to the boy. *Lord, please let this be the one.*

Around them Radu and Anika unpacked the car. "Come in where it's warm." Anika chased them inside.

"Can the children open their presents right away?" Carrie begged. "I can't wait another minute!" Excitement flooded her cheeks with a gentle pink. Anika nodded.

The stack of presents looked pitifully small. Steve thought of the hoard of gifts surrounding the tree at Tim and Brenda's house, enough to line an entire wall. No wonder the rest of the world thought Americans were rich. Watching Carrie's irrepressible anticipation, Steve realized these children were rich in the most important thing, their "mother's" love.

"Shall we do this one at a time or all at once?" Carrie's lips twisted in a thoughtful scowl. "All at once, I think. Keep them from fighting over each other's toys." She picked through the presents. "Adrian." She handed the boy a round-shaped package that could only be a ball. "Jenica. Octavia." Two rectangular-shaped boxes. "Ion." A long narrow package.

"Viktor." Her voice reflected the gleeful satisfaction of knowing the gift was just right.

Carrie sat down to wait and watch the fun. Jenica fingered the bright paper, but the other children didn't touch their gifts.

Ion started coughing. Octavia stared around the crowded room and began crying.

"They don't know what to do." Carrie spoke in a surprised undertone. A flickering second of sadness passed over her face. Steve found himself missing her almost naive smile and hurried to help.

"Viktor. Come here." The boy looked up but didn't move. *Of course, he doesn't speak English.* Steve settled himself on the floor next to the child. "You do it like this." He hooked a finger under the edge of the wrapping paper and started to pull. Viktor watched then looked into Steve's eyes. "Your turn." Steve guided the child's hands into the opening, and together they tore away the paper to reveal a slender box. Steve pried open the end flaps and pulled out the present—a white plastic recorder. Viktor's eyes fixed on him, as if demanding an explanation.

"Listen!" Steve put the instrument to his mouth and blew a note. The boy drew back, startled. The adults laughed. "You try it." Steve handed the recorder to the child.

Viktor held the instrument in his hands, fingering the holes, chewing on the edge, and eventually put the mouthpiece to his lips. He puffed out his cheeks and blew. A squeaky note emerged.

"Bravo!" Carrie applauded. "That's the way!"

Another squeak followed. A series of them, all high pitched. Recorder clamped in his mouth, Viktor looked like he would play forever.

"May I?" Steve reached for the recorder. Viktor scowled at him and bit down on the mouthpiece.

"You do it like this." Steve knelt in front of the child and molded his fingers over the holes. Surprise flit across Viktor's face when the next note came out an octave lower. Soon he was blowing an experimental series of notes up and down the scale.

The rest of the morning flew by. The children clustered around Carrie, at least three of them occupying her lap at all times. She talked to them constantly, short sentences illustrated by gestures, certain words repeated often enough that Steve could guess their meanings—the color red, the number two. Fixing a bottle, changing a diaper, helping open a present—for two hours she never stopped moving.

Soon only a few presents remained. "For you, Carrie," Anika announced.

Steve hugged himself with delight at the surprised look on her face. *I hope she likes it!*

Almost reverently she pulled aside the tissue paper and opened the drawstrings of a soft cloth bag to reveal a bottle of hand lotion and a big bar of scented soap. Closing her eyes, she lifted the soap to her nose and sniffed deeply, sighing with pleasure. "Gardenias. Summer in the middle of winter." She looked at him with warm brown eyes.

"Brenda—my sister, you know—loves it. She complains about chafed hands—"

"It's wonderful. But I don't have anything for you!" Carrie pumped a minuscule amount of lotion onto Jenica and Octavia's outstretched hands before rubbing it into her own.

"That's okay." *But you already have given me something. Your warmth. Time with these children.*

Presents from their hosts followed, a cassette of folk songs for Steve and for Carrie, an intricately executed Tree of Jesse, the size of a sheet of notebook paper.

"How beautiful!" She traced the branches leading from Jesse to Jesus. "And there shall come forth a rod out of the stem of Jesse. . ." She clutched it to her chest. "Thank you, Lord." After a few moments she slid it back inside the envelope and set it aside, out of reach of the children.

"Good." Radu and Anika wore matching beaming smiles.

They shared the closeness of a happily married couple. The love between Carrie and the children bonded them in a different kind of family. A pang of loneliness akin to jealousy crossed Steve's heart. *Be patient,* he tried to console himself. *God makes everything beautiful in His time.*

❧

"I'll take care of the children." Anika practically pushed Carrie out the door. "Go with Radu and Steve to church."

They'll be okay. Carrie steeled herself to withstand Octavia's wails and Ion's nose, going like a runaway train. Anika pulled Adrian back from where he clutched Carrie's pant leg.

"I'll be right back." She gave each child a quick hug and kiss. Thanking Anika, she walked out into the snowstorm.

On the sidewalk Steve and Radu stood waiting. Steve's ears burned red, begging for a covering. She adjusted the warm beret on her head. White snow blurred the outlines of buildings, creating a festive fairyland where anything could happen. Steve trudged next to her, immersed in his own world. He looked like he had lost weight, creating interesting angles in his facial bones that emphasized the loneliness lurking within.

What's he been doing for the last year? And why does he want to adopt? She had to admire a man who would spend a small fortune traveling halfway across the world to adopt a child. He was brave, all right. *But does he know what he's getting into?* Around the kids he acted slow and wooden. The old Steve, the one with a ready chuckle and a smile that could warm an entire room, stayed hidden most of the time. Now and then some of the old sparkle appeared, like when he showed Viktor how to play the recorder.

Inside she grinned. Who wouldn't warm up to Viktor? She loved him like he was her own.

Why not? The thought popped into Carrie's head like the scent of hot cocoa. *If they let single parents like Steve adopt, why not me?* The thought fit exactly, instantly taking hold.

She'd probably have to complete an adoption application. It couldn't be any worse than the mission society form. She could already imagine the future. Through a snowy looking glass, she dreamed of Christmases to come. Viktor gamboled in the ball pit at a McDonald's playland. Red backpack strapped to his back and Big Bird smiling on his shirt, Viktor walked with her to kindergarten. A shadowy figure marched in band, playing an instrument. Was it a clarinet? No, a trumpet.

Ahead of her the men had stopped, and she realized they had arrived at the church.

"Any luck with your search?" Radu asked Steve while he unlocked the door.

"Yes." Steve paused before saying more. Conflicting emotions flashed across his face.

"Really? Who?" Full of her own plans, Carrie longed to share his joy.

He glanced at Carrie then answered. "Viktor. I want to adopt Viktor."

eight

"He's going to take Viktor!" Unable to believe it, Carrie spouted to Michelle at their next lunch meeting. "Thousands of children to choose from, and he wants Viktor!" She dabbed at the angry tears she knew she had no right to cry.

"Well, that's good, isn't it?" Michelle sounded bewildered. "That way you know Viktor has a good future. Why, you might even get to see him sometime." Her attempt at empathy failed.

"You don't understand." Tears flowed in earnest now. "I had just decided. I was hoping. I was going to try to adopt Viktor myself."

Surprised silence followed. "But could you?" Michelle had obviously never considered the possibility. "Adopt, I mean?"

"Why not?" Carrie threw her head back in defiance. "If they let a single man like Steve-stick-in-the-mud-Romero adopt, why not me?"

Michelle's expression suggested that she could think of several reasons, but she didn't mention any of them. Instead her eyes softened. "No wonder you're disappointed."

They sipped their coffee in silence. "He may still change his mind." Michelle attempted to console her friend.

"I don't think so." Carrie shook her head. "You should have seen them together on Christmas Day."

"I'll see what I can find out when we go to dinner." Michelle grinned at Carrie's surprise. "You know I'm a sucker for that hangdog look."

Carrie tried to ignore the feeling of jealousy that clogged her throat and increased the tension one more notch. She wanted, no, needed, to talk with Sister Pauline. A conversation with the wise old woman would clear up some of her confusion.

That evening Carrie walked around the wards with the director. The children, the atmosphere, the smells, all disappeared as she poured out her heart.

"And so I decided I would like to adopt. I thought about Viktor." Carrie swallowed past the lump in her throat. "But if that isn't possible, one of the others."

Sister Pauline didn't answer but continued her routine, making sure every child had a bottle or blanket or whatever else was needed. After finishing the evening round, she took Carrie with her to the chapel.

"Let us pray together about your desires." Her words reminded Carrie that she had not prayed before making her new plans.

Of course it's God's will. How can it not be? At the prayer rail, Carrie lifted her hands in silent supplication. *If it is Your will, let me adopt Viktor. Please. Or show me which of the others is the one You want for me.* Her mind raced ahead of her prayers, and she found it hard to focus.

Candles burned low before Pauline rose from her knees.

"Sit down." Her face was at peace as she settled next to Carrie on the pew. "My dear child."

I wish she wouldn't call me that. It usually signaled bad news.

❧

"Have you thought this through?" A thin hand gripped Carrie's arm. "The Lord has given you a great love for children and a tremendous gift for working with them. But are you prepared to take responsibility for one child's life from now until eternity? To provide for his physical needs and guide his spiritual growth?"

Why is she asking? Carrie frowned. "Of course!"

Sister Pauline sighed, as if disappointed in Carrie's answer. "I will help you complete the necessary paperwork, if that is what you wish." She stood, indicating the discussion had ended.

"Don't be weary in well doing," she said, quoting from Galatians. "Don't let your enthusiasm keep you from completing your work here." They parted ways at the door.

Carrie settled into bed for the night, somewhat puzzled and disappointed. Sister Pauline hadn't exactly encouraged her. *Am I doing the right thing? Isn't adopting a child just an extension of my calling to Romania?* She turned over and punched her pillow, chasing away the doubts. *Of course it is.*

❧

Steve paused at the door, questioning the wisdom of taking Michelle to dinner. At the time, the arrangement happened naturally. He needed a break from the inevitable letdown following the surge of discovery. She knew where to go for an American meal. Just like home, she promised. Later, he wondered if she was thinking "date." He shrugged. If so, that was her problem.

She arrived promptly—well, only fifteen minutes late. Dressed in typical college fashion, with makeup carefully applied, she gleamed with a purely American beauty. At the same time she soothed his loneliness in a foreign country and defined her expectations of the evening.

Maybe it's time, Steve decided. After all, his last date, before his engagement, had been four and a half years ago. Lila had been as comfortable as a worn glove. He didn't know how to begin with Michelle. Now if it were Carrie, it wouldn't be so hard.

Summoning a forgotten skill, he searched for an opening comment. Of course, a compliment. "You look lovely. That sweater—"

"Oh, this old thing. It must be out of date by now." She giggled nervously, but she was clearly pleased.

The restaurant proved to be everything she had promised. Large chandeliers illuminated tables covered with sparkling white linen; napkins were folded into tents on bread and butter plates. The menu, written in English, featured American favorites like T-bone steaks and fried chicken.

Michelle stared at him over the top of the menu.

"What do you recommend?"

She hesitated. *Price*, he realized. It was up to him to set the standard. "Uh, is the steak any good?"

"Yes, as long as you like it cooked somewhere between well done and burned tough!"

"Sounds—perfect!" He could eat decent American steak in Denver any time. Orders placed, an uncomfortable silence descended on the table. *I've forgotten how to make small talk, at least with someone besides band students and parents.* He looked at Michelle over the candles, and she smiled at him with orthodontist-straightened teeth. Her youthful idealism multiplied the five or so years' difference in their ages. The silence lengthened as the waiter brought salads to the table.

Michelle began telling him how she ended up in Bucharest. *Why did Carrie return?* Was it as complicated as Michelle's story sounded? Knowing Carrie, he suspected she jumped right in without much thought.

Michelle mentioned meeting with Carrie every Thursday and then started describing the ladies' Bible study she had organized.

"How is it going?" He tried to hold up his end of the conversation.

She beamed with pleasure, as if she had been waiting for some show of interest on his part. "Five women came last week. They're so hungry for God's Word! I guess I've taken it too much for granted." She was off and running again.

The one-sided monologue prompted by occasional questions from Steve lasted through the main course. Half an ear paying attention to Michelle, Steve found himself wondering if he could complete the adoption process before he had to return home after the new year.

They ordered dessert, a hot fudge sundae for Steve and apple pie à la mode for Michelle. "I've monopolized the conversation," she apologized. "Tell me about yourself. I hear you've decided to adopt Viktor. Carrie's just crazy about him. I suppose you know that."

"Yes." Tongue-tied, he didn't say any more. How could he explain the visions of the boy in his nursery in Denver, playing with Sammy and Amanda?

"How long will you be staying in Romania?" A pretty blush stained Michelle's cheeks, as if she were asking for herself.

"One more week. School starts again next Tuesday."

The waiter arrived, and the vanilla ice cream proved rich, buttery, and creamy. Steve let it slide down his throat.

"Only a week? Then when are you coming back?" Michelle returned to their conversation.

"Coming back?" Her words reminded him of the obstacles ahead, and the ice cream landed with a cold lump at the back of his throat. "I guess I've been hoping for the impossible, to cut through all the red tape."

"Someone at the agency must have told you. It takes months, years, even, to get a child out of Romania." She swallowed a juicy bite of pie. "Viktor may be old enough for school before you finish the process."

She pointed a finger at him. "First, have you got permission to adopt Viktor from his parents?"

Parents? He's at an orphanage.

A second finger jabbed. "Also, has he been tested for HIV yet?"

HIV? As in AIDS? He had forgotten about that part. It was too horrible to contemplate.

As if sensing his confusion, she explained. "A lot of babies were infected when they received a blood transfusion at birth, a routine practice in Romania. As many as forty percent in some places. And any child that tests positive isn't allowed into the United States."

Sighing, she lifted another finger. "Then of course there are all the papers to be prepared and translated."

Steve stirred in his chair. "I've contacted a lawyer here. He's already done most of that."

"And signed by the president. If he signs them at all."

"I guess I was dreaming." Steve slumped, leaving the last spoonful of fudge sauce untouched. She was right. He could not possibly finish everything in under a week. It had been foolish to think he could. Another dead end? Discouragement swamped him, and he slid a couple of inches in his chair.

Michelle resumed her monologue, now sharing humorous vignettes of an American abroad, kindly not seeming to notice as he withdrew further into himself. Finally he shook out of his funk. If it was possible to make the adoption happen faster, he would. He dug out the last spoonful of the now-melted ice cream, and the waiter reappeared with the coffeepot. "Not for me. It would keep me awake all night."

Michelle took her cue from him. "Me neither. I am a bit tired. Mind if we leave?"

"Of course."

She bustled them out of the restaurant and delivered him at Radu's apartment with surprising speed. Before he could get out of the car, she placed a warm hand on his arm. "I do hope you get to take Viktor home soon. We're here to help—Radu, Anika, Carrie, me—if you need us."

Michelle's words echoed in Steve's mind. Phone dangling from his hands, he started to dial Carrie's number. *Don't call.* The phone slipped into the cradle. He was sure Radu would go with him. Perhaps he would be a better advocate than another American, even if she did know the boy and speak Romanian.

Call her. Hesitating, Steve picked up the receiver again and stared at it. Radu didn't love the boy like Carrie did. She would make an impassioned plea on his behalf.

Or would she? Would she let her attachment to Viktor stand in the way? There was only one way to find out.

Somewhere close by a clock chimed ten. *It's probably her bedtime.* He tapped the receiver against the table. It might be the best time to reach her.

Drawing a deep breath, he dialed the number given him by Radu. Ten, twenty rings later, a childish voice answered. "Hello?"

"I'd like to speak with Carrie Randolph, please. Car—rie Ran—dolph." Steve tried to slow down his natural speech and say the name clearly.

"Okay." A loud bump rang in his ear, and he heard footsteps slapping across a wooden floor. Had she understood? The second hand moved slowly on his watch dial, time Steve spent trying to curb his impatience. Eventually the clatter of nearing footsteps rewarded his wait.

"This is Carrie Randolph." She sounded breathless, as if she had been running.

"Carrie. This is Steve Romero."

"Steve!" Her voice conveyed genuine warmth. After a second's pause, she asked, "How is the adoption coming?" Only a slight quiver in her voice betrayed any ambivalence.

"Actually, that's why I'm calling. I understand I need to get permission from Viktor's parents before I can go further. Do you know if they're still alive? Or is he really orphaned?"

A brief silence followed. "They're alive. They live in a village north of Bucharest."

"Well." Steve cut off the word. Whenever he was nervous, his voice took on an impersonal business tone. The illusion of control worked well with high school students. *How will it go over with Carrie? Better be real.*

"I could use your help. I'm afraid I might do something to offend someone unintentionally. Could you come with me when I go to visit Viktor's parents?" Steve pictured Carrie, head pinning phone to her shoulder and chewing on her lower lip.

"I'll have to check with Sister Pauline. But I'd be glad to help if I can." She answered without hesitation.

"Tomorrow? Or the day after? I don't have much time—I have to return to Denver soon."

"Plan on the day after tomorrow. New Year's Eve."

Steve glanced at the calendar. That would be Thursday, Carrie's day off. His heart swelled with gratitude for her generosity.

"Thanks." They made plans and hung up the phone.

❧

"It's about ninety kilometers from here. A tad over fifty-five miles." Excitement laced with nervousness pounded through Carrie's veins as she drove to the village where Viktor's parents lived. The horizon gleamed white and cold, an unpromising backdrop to the day. Soon the city dropped out of sight, and paved roads gave way to frozen dirt, bouncing the vehicle around like a boat at sea. Empty brown fields sidelined the path, with occasional clusters of buildings indicating a village.

Carrie darted glances at Steve. Close-clipped curls hugged his face and drew attention to his sensitive mouth. It was the face of someone she would like to know better. He had changed since Lila's death. If only he didn't want to adopt Viktor! Her stomach tightened at the thought of the upcoming meeting. If Steve was nervous about the day's errand, he didn't show it.

She shifted her gaze to the undulating road. Hopefully her demeanor was as unrevealing. The bottom line was that she hoped Viktor's parents would agree to the adoption.

She checked the odometer as another village came into view. "This should be the place." A dozen buildings identified the center of town, and an assortment of farm animals roamed about. Brown earth enclosed by white fences outlined garden plots that would flourish with vegetables come spring.

She stopped the car and rolled down the window.

"Where do the Grozas live?" she asked in Romanian of a woman passing by, carrying buckets of water.

"Over there." Only her eyes registered surprise at the arrival of Americans in her village.

Carrie thought she had grown immune to Romania's poverty, but the house still surprised her. The records indicated Viktor was the youngest of eleven children. The cottage couldn't be larger than seven hundred square feet. How could twelve people live in such a small place? She eased the car off the road, feeling ice crush and wheels sink into partially frozen mud.

"Just a minute." Steve's face was pale, his words shaky. He was nervous, after all. "Let's pray."

"Of course!" When would she learn? Always rushing ahead, she kept neglecting to talk with God about things.

"God, give me the words to say." As Steve bent over, head clasped between his hands, Carrie hurriedly closed her eyes. "Open the Grozas' hearts. Help me to accept whatever happens today." His voice quavered, and he didn't say anything more for a few seconds.

Words failed Carrie. She didn't know what to pray for. After a quick silent confession of her desire to keep Viktor for herself, she simply added, "We trust You to do what is best for Viktor."

"Amen." Steve concluded the prayer. "Let's go."

Dozens of eyes peered at Carrie when she looked up. A group of children stood at a respectful distance around the car, staring at them in curiosity. Viktor's bright black eyes and the bump at the end of his nose repeated themselves in the faces. Addressing the oldest, she asked in Romanian, "May we see Mr. and Mrs. Groza?"

The girl disappeared inside the cottage and reappeared a moment later with a thin, wiry woman, clearly every ounce a scrapper. She approached the car. "I am Mrs. Groza."

Carrie's mouth turned to cotton. They hadn't discussed an

opening gambit. How could they explain their mission? At her side Steve stirred uneasily, clearing his throat. The woman made it easy. "Come inside."

Carrie gestured for Steve to follow her into the cramped cottage. Dishes, clothes, and furniture filled every inch, neatly squeezed into place.

"You are from the children's home." Mrs. Groza saved them from introducing themselves. "I recognize the car. Has something happened to my Viktor? Is he well?" Her anxious words and worry lines tightening her eyes hinted at a wealth of mother love Carrie could only approximate.

Steve stirred at the mention of Viktor, and Carrie translated for him.

"He is fine. In fact, we have some wonderful news." Carrie glanced at Steve, who nodded his encouragement. "This gentleman here, Steve Romero"—he smiled at the mention of his name—"is from the United States. He is interested in adopting Viktor and taking him to live in America."

The shocked mask that covered Mrs. Groza's face didn't need translation. "Wait a minute. I must call my husband."

A quarter of an hour later, the four of them faced each other across the crowded room. Once again Carrie explained their errand.

"No." Mr. Groza spoke without hesitation. "We believe things will get better soon. We will be able to bring our son home."

Carrie swallowed a protest. *Who does he think he's fooling?* She thought of the stick-thin children outside and the cramped conditions of the home.

"He says no," she said to Steve, trying to keep disappointment out of her voice.

"But Mr. Groza. . ." Without waiting for Carrie to translate, Steve pulled out a book of snapshots. Words and pleas spewed out as he hurried to convince them.

"This is my home. See, this is the nursery. Viktor will have it all to himself. Here is my piano. Viktor loves music, you know. I could teach him."

Carrie inserted an explanation here and there but mostly let the pictures speak for themselves. Steve continued urging the advantages of life in America. Caught up in his plea, he appeared not to notice the way Mr. Groza drew back and sank into his chair.

"The answer is still no."

Shaking her head, Carrie communicated his refusal to Steve. Silence reigned. She hated to see him hurt like this.

❧

"Wait." Viktor's mother leafed through Steve's pictures and pointed to a view of him in front of a church. "You are a Christian?" She pointed to her only piece of jewelry, a simple cross necklace.

"Yes."

They had found common ground.

Mrs. Groza put a hand on her husband's knee. "That is good. The reason we took Viktor to Sister Pauline, instead of somewhere else, was so he could learn about our Lord."

Carrie explained to Steve. Mrs. Groza clutched her husband's hand, and he slowly nodded.

They looked at Steve with gazes full of a lifetime of pain that pierced Carrie's soul. "Now God has brought you here. You would teach our son about the Lord." She reached for the pen in Steve's hand. "We will sign the papers." Tears smeared the ink of their signatures.

Steve took pictures of Viktor's family and their home. "I will tell him about his parents, who loved him very much," he promised.

Mrs. Groza handed Steve a cloth-wrapped bundle. "Keep this for my son."

"May I?" Steve unfolded the material, revealing a well-worn Bible. "He will treasure this." His voice broke.

Carrie didn't speak much on the trip back to the home. The unselfish, painful sacrifice of Viktor's parents bore down on her, hammering her resistance to Steve's desire to adopt her favorite. *Do I love him that much? Enough to give him up?* The bleak winter landscape offered no easy answers.

Steve made up for her silence, talking nonstop like a toy that wouldn't wind down. How God had led him step by step to Viktor, and his conviction that everything else would work out. How he looked forward to having a son to cherish, to share life with.

Carrie concentrated on driving and let his words slide off without penetrating. Her thought followed a separate path. *If not Viktor, could I adopt one of the others? Adrian, perhaps?* Dark had fallen when they reached the home. Soon, she promised herself, soon she would be rejoicing the same way.

"Wait!" Steve stopped Carrie before she could get out of the car. Jumping out his side, he ran around and opened her door with a flourish. He leaned in and kissed her cheek. "Thanks for everything. I know how much Viktor means to you." Taking her arm by the elbow, he walked her to the door. "I know there's a lot left to do, more red tape. I want to spend as much time as possible with Viktor before I leave. Do you mind if I come tomorrow?"

Carrie automatically made arrangements. Glad to see him leave, she headed for the toddler ward. Perhaps a brief good night greeting would restore her sagging spirits.

Sister Marie dozed in her chair, and Carrie opened the door without disturbing her. She tiptoed past the cribs. At the far end, Ion's breathing rasped. Octavia twisted in her sleep as if she were having a vivid dream. Thumb in mouth, Jenica slept peacefully. Carrie tugged a blanket over her, stroking her soft hair and skin. Tears watered her cheeks. With or without Viktor, there were plenty of reasons to be in Romania. Adrian. She smiled and headed for his crib next.

From a few feet away, the mattress looked flat, no familiar lumpy figure visible. Her footsteps quickened, and she stopped worrying about making noise as she rushed to the bed—empty. Adrian was gone.

She ran out the door and shook Sister Marie awake. "Where is Adrian?"

The woman stirred and blinked eyes against the light. "Adrian? They took him away today."

"What? Who?" Panicked, Carrie realized Marie didn't know the answer. She raced down the stairs and to the main house, barreling down the hall to Sister Pauline's door. The director stood waiting, petite form outlined by the dim light.

"Come in, dear child."

"Where is Adrian?"

Sister Pauline did not answer until they sat down facing each other. Clasping Carrie's hand between her own, she said, "Adrian came to us because his mother was young and unmarried. She always hoped she could take care of him when her circumstances changed."

"So?"

"She came today. She has married now, and her husband has a good job in the city. He is willing to raise Adrian as his own. They left just before supper."

Nooo! I didn't even get to say good-bye! Carrie looked at the floor, away from the compassion shining in Sister Pauline's eyes.

"It is for the best, you know."

Without answering, Carrie rose from her chair and stumbled down the hall into her room and collapsed on her bed. In the privacy of her room, she allowed the tears to fall. *Who knew a happy ending could hurt so much?*

nine

With a whistle streaming between his teeth, Steve burst through the door and up the stairs to the toddler ward. He didn't want to waste a moment he could spend with Viktor. And Carrie—she had a way of making him relax. If only he could speed up the rest of the bureaucratic process. Oh, well, after six years of touring with the Singers, he knew how time consuming and inflexible government protocol could be.

Carrie was nowhere to be seen. Sister Marie smiled at him and pointed toward a door at the opposite end of the ward. Surprised that Carrie and the children weren't waiting for him, he knocked on the door.

"Come in."

A giggling Jenica stood before Carrie, wrapped in a thin towel that Carrie rubbed briskly against skin and hair. Three more heads bobbed in and out of the bath water, with a generous portion spreading across the floor.

"Rough morning, huh?" He chuckled. "How can I help?"

"Their baths are finished. Just need to get them dried off and dressed. The clothes are over there."

Steve looked for Viktor's head in the swishing water. There he was. He seemed to recognize Steve, a shy smile acknowledging his presence as he lifted the boy out of the tub.

"Hi there, Viktor." He held the towel-garbed boy close for a moment and took a second look at the tub. Someone was missing. "Where's Adrian this morning?"

"He's gone." Carrie pulled a shirt over Jenica's head and reached for Octavia. "His mother came to take him home yesterday while we were gone."

To someone who had so recently lost his own child, Carrie's grief was almost palpable. He stopped drying Viktor. "I'm sorry."

"No need to be sorry." Carrie brushed at the corners of her eyes and searched for matching socks. "It's what's best for him. Back with his family."

"Yes," Steve acknowledged. "But it must still hurt."

Tiny lines tightened around eyes brimming with tears. His heart went out to her, knowing the pain that came with losing a child. Without thinking, he extended his arms to embrace her, cradling her head against his shoulder, letting her tears soak into his shirt.

Ion sneezed, and Carrie instantly straightened. "What must you think of me. Look at your shirt. And the children."

"It's all right." Steve handed her a dry handkerchief. Comforting Carrie felt as natural as drying his sister's tears after her first boyfriend dropped her.

On the other hand, Carrie seemed embarrassed. Her actions sped into hyperdrive, whipping Jenica and Ion into clothes while Steve struggled to pin on a cloth diaper.

Viktor was still only half dressed when Carrie finished. "You need help with that?" Her amusement seemed to hold a trace of contempt at his ineptitude.

"Well." He flashed a sheepish grin in her direction. "Yes. I'm used to disposable diapers."

"Okay. You do it like this." She trifolded the cloth and pinned it snugly in place in a few seconds. Clothes followed in a matter of minutes. "There."

"Thanks." *How am I ever going to manage a child on my own? Practice, I suppose. All new parents have to learn sometime.* Remembering Tim's stories of 2:00 a.m. bottle feedings, he was glad Viktor was past the feed-me-every-two-hours stage.

Together they cleaned the bathroom, soaking up the water that splashed, taking the wet towels and discarded clothes to the laundry—the towels were so thin, Steve feared they might fall apart in the wash—and headed down the stairs.

Steve glanced over his shoulder from the bottom and grinned at the picture. The children carefully climbed the steps, maneuvering the stairs with about as much skill as a pull toy. At the back, Carrie held Octavia's hand, heavy diaper bag dragging down her shoulder.

"Let me carry that." How thoughtless he must seem, leaving everything for her to carry.

"I'm used to it."

I'm sure you are. Ignoring her comment, he climbed the steps two at a time and slid the bag down her arm into his hands.

"Where are we headed?" Carrie managed to raise a wan smile when they reached the car.

"My surprise." He tucked the children in back. Apparently no laws here governed safety belts and child seats. *What a ridiculous notion.* Danger to Romania's children came from more basic sources like starvation and lack of medical care.

"How about some songs to pass the time?" he suggested. "You lead. I haven't sung too many nursery rhymes lately." That wasn't entirely true—he read Mother Goose to Sammy and Amanda all the time—but he wanted to get Carrie's mind off Adrian. She started to sing in a lovely soprano voice.

"Hey Diddle Diddle" followed "Twinkle, Twinkle, Little Star." *It's working.* Laughter lines erased the grief in Carrie's face as she clapped along.

"I wish I knew Romanian rhymes," she confessed. "The only songs I know are in English."

"Try something universal, then. Like animal songs." He started "Old McDonald" and meowed.

"Cat." Jenica spoke up for the first time.

"Good for you!" Carrie grinned widely. Soon they were all singing along, a mixture of English and Romanian and animalese.

Country roads gave way to the busy city. Steve stopped singing and concentrated on following the directions Michelle had supplied. Soon familiar golden arches appeared.

"McDonald's!" Carrie exclaimed, delighted.

"Complete with a playland," Steve announced proudly. "Michelle told me about it."

Children's meals in hand, they took their lunches to the playroom. The children stared at the yellow and red ropes and slides. A couple of toddlers romped in the ball pit. Babies crawled, heads barely showing above the balls. Older children dove in, splashing orbs in every direction, some landing outside the net. A bright red ball rolled toward Octavia, a blue one to Viktor.

Solemn, Octavia carried the ball back to the net and pushed it through. A little girl in a Cinderella shirt waved to the group. "Come in." When they didn't climb in, she returned to her play.

Gradually the children drew in a tightening circle around the play equipment, still not quite daring to join in.

A couple settled in next to where Steve and Carrie apportioned the children's meals.

"Janie! Come eat!" The Cinderella girl reluctantly left the toys.

"Just visiting?" Carrie inquired.

"You're American!" The woman said with evident relief. "Yes, we're visiting family. But Janie has been dragging us back here every day since she discovered there was a McDonald's nearby."

For the next few minutes everyone concentrated on eating. Steve tore open a ketchup packet, squeezed it on Viktor's fries, and fed one into his mouth. His bright eyes widened in delight, and soon he was stuffing them in for himself.

Jenica slurped down her drink. Ion took apart his hamburger, trying pickles, bread, and meat separately. Within minutes it was impossible to tell any of them had taken a bath. Steve wondered if Carrie would resent the extra work.

"You can tell we don't do this very often." She looked at the mess they had made. "But what fun!"

"Birthday party? Or are they all yours?" The American mother asked in an unbelieving voice as she passed by their table on the way to the trash can.

"Neither." Carrie blushed. "They're all from a children's home, where I do volunteer work."

A solemn, oh-those-poor-children expression transformed the mother's face.

"And I'm hoping to adopt." Steve stated while he wiped Viktor's face and hands clean with a moist cloth.

"Congratulations!" A smile replaced the frown. "It's just that you looked so natural together."

The girl tugged on her mother's arm and whispered in her ear. "Of course," the mother responded.

"Come play with me," Janie invited, taking Viktor's hand. He followed as she tugged him toward the playground, looking over his shoulder at Carrie and Steve, uncertain what he should do.

Carrie fell in behind with Ion and Octavia. The children followed Janie's lead, climbing through the narrow opening into the ball pit. "Come on, Jenica," she invited. Soon five heads were bobbing up like buoys on the ocean.

"Thank you," Carrie told the mother. "Janie can show them how to play." A warm smile erased the grief Steve had seen earlier as they watched a giggling Jenica pitch a ball in Ion's direction.

Steve feasted his eyes on the sight of Viktor bouncing among the balls and falling against the ropes. How good to see him enjoying a few moments of carefree childhood, something Americans tended to forget was not the birthright of every child born in the world. There was so much he wanted to do and so little time to do it in. If Lila were here, she could stay when he had to return to his job, deal with the paperwork, and get Viktor home sooner.

If Lila were alive, I wouldn't be in Romania adopting Viktor. That was then; this is now. Viktor is my future.

Steve looked at Carrie, wondering if she was enjoying the day as much as he was. A worry arrow arched between her eyebrows, and tears glistened in her eyes.

"Adrian?" he asked softly.

She nodded. "He would have loved it here." She looked at her watch. "I hate to say it, but—"

"It's time to go."

The children slipped down the slide into their waiting arms, grins lighting their faces. Clean faces and hands and changed diapers later, they were on their way.

❧

Steve made a snap decision. "I want to make a stop," he told Carrie, steering the car toward Radu's apartment. He darted in and gathered together some of the supplies he had brought with him from Denver. Storing them out of sight in the trunk, he climbed behind the wheel and headed back to the home.

The motion of the car lulled the children to sleep, and Carrie leaned back against the headrest, eyes closed. "Thanks. What a wonderful day." Her head drooped against her chest.

In glances, Steve studied her profile, her face peaceful in repose, her body pleasantly curved. A nice girl. He hoped they could keep in touch, through Victory Singers reunions or something. He'd like to see how she turned out. He could envision her with a family of her own, three or four children. An unexpected pang of jealousy crossed his heart when he imagined her family—children and father and mother together.

Before long the car pulled up beside the toddler ward. Steve helped settle the children in their cribs.

"Thank you again."

"There's one more thing. Come with me to my car." Opening the trunk, he extracted half a dozen packages of disposable diapers and shoved them at a surprised Carrie.

"I brought them with me, just in case," he explained. "No point in lugging them back to Denver. They might make your life easier now and again."

"Oh, wow." She threaded her hands through the bag handles as if they were strings of pearls. "Thanks! See you tomorrow?"

"I wouldn't miss it!"

Two short days later, Carrie accompanied Steve and Radu to the airport with Viktor and the other children. Steve wasn't sure he wanted Viktor to be there. Saying good-bye the previous night had been tough. Today, in full view of an airport full of people, would be close to impossible.

The children behaved well, too well. Unlike Sammy and Amanda who fidgeted within minutes of arriving at the departure gate, they were too withdrawn to get restless and bored in the confined lounge area.

Steve held Viktor in his lap, savoring the fit of his body in his arms and the brush of his hair against his chin.

"So when do you think you'll be back?" Radu asked.

"Probably summer. Spring break lasts only a week, not enough time to finish everything."

The intercom cackled, and Carrie stood up. "That's your flight."

Steve stood up, holding on to Viktor. The boy nestled against Steve's chest, questions arising in his dark eyes. The thought of leaving him behind for six months sickened Steve. No matter how valid the reason, his departure betrayed the trust Viktor placed in him.

Now I understand. Pauline had counseled against informing Viktor about his plans. So many things could still go wrong, and six months was an eternity to a young child. Less disappointment for both him and Viktor if things didn't work out.

But of course they will. It's just a matter of time. Have patience. This summer. Trying to keep tears from spilling out and upsetting the children, Steve gently squeezed Viktor and kissed the top of his head before handing him over to Carrie.

"I guess this is good-bye, then." Steve shook Radu's hand.

"Not good-bye. Until next time."

"Don't worry. I'll take good care of him for you," Carrie promised.

"I'm sure of that." Unable to grasp her hand—she was holding Viktor—Steve patted her shoulder instead and walked away. If possible, he felt lonelier than he did on the first half of his trip. He had hoped to not return alone.

❧

Steve ran his fingers over the raised letters of the nameplate now hanging on the nursery door: V-I-K-T-O-R. God willing, he would be victorious in bringing his son home come summer.

Spring light bathed the room in a warm glow when he opened the door. Toddler toys filled the room, treasures found in his new passion for garage sales. He couldn't pass one without stopping for a look. Walking and riding toys dominated. His favorite find was a musical rocking horse, painted and polished to gleaming newness.

A snapshot of Viktor stood on the dresser, with a well-read letter from Carrie lying beside it. "He is doing well. He survived the winter without colds," she reported. "The pictures you send attract attention from all the other toddlers. In caring for Viktor, you are doing good for everyone here."

Should I go back during spring break? He argued with himself for the hundredth time. It didn't make any sense, but he would have a chance to see Viktor for a few more days. *And Carrie.* Missing both of them, he pressed the play button on his tape recorder and listened to Carrie speak about Viktor's progress with his instrument. Viktor's piping voice and fluting melody filled the empty silence. He kissed the picture frame. "Oh, Lord, let it be soon," he entreated.

❧

A bird Carrie didn't recognize built a nest under the eaves. Tiny peeping voices greeted Carrie morning by morning and spring progressed. She studied the shadow of the intricately woven nest barely discernible against the dark walls.

Soon the nestlings would fly solo, abandoning their parents. Did birds feel as bereft as she did at the prospect of watching Viktor leave? His face hovered in her mind, and she allowed herself the luxury of a moment of regret.

Today marked another step in the process: HIV testing. Ion, Octavia, Jenica, and newcomer Angelica would be checked as well. Just in case, she wanted to pave the way for her own attempts to adopt.

I'm worried about Ion, she mused as she walked toward the ward. His cough persisted into the milder spring weather. Wasn't an inability to heal a sign of AIDS?

First stop—Adrian's old crib, now occupied by Angelica, a sweet girl with crippled legs. She was the physical opposite of her predecessor. Brought in by a mother who couldn't continue the level of care required by her disabled daughter, at least she knew how to smile and talk and yes, cry, in grief and anger.

Carrie didn't begrudge a minute of the extra time Angelica required. With her welcoming cry of "Carrie!" (not "Mama," like the other children called her), her spontaneous laugh when a soap bubble burst in her face, Angelica abounded in small moments of joy that gave Carrie the strength she needed to keep trying with the other four.

Next Carrie lifted Viktor down, careful not to disturb the snapshots of him with Steve and the colorful postcards that arrived on a regular basis. An older one was falling off. Carrie reread the familiar message before sticking it back on the crib. Viktor's thumbprints nearly obliterated the words. "This is Buffalo Bill, a famous American cowboy. I hope you can visit his house some day." A picture of the blond-haired, mustached entertainer stared at her. Apparently his gravesite was near Denver.

Carrie sighed. Although she would never admit it to anyone else, she looked forward to seeing Steve again. Viktor connected them in a tight bond. After all, Steve would soon officially be his father, and wasn't she like his mother?

Stop fantasizing. You can't have Viktor. Pick a different child.

No word had arrived yet on her application. *What's taking so long?* she wondered as she helped Octavia out of her crib. The child scampered across the floor toward the bath, bringing a smile to Carrie's face. She was definitely gaining strength, even if her legs stayed thin as string, too thin it seemed to support her ever-lengthening body.

After a hurried bath and rushed breakfast, it was time to meet with Dr. Reynaud at the clinic that Cristina had bragged about on Carrie's first visit.

The doctor visited at least once a quarter, helping the most desperately ill children and seeking to ease the way for American and French couples trying to adopt. An older, Gallic version of Brad Pitt, he flirted outright with Carrie.

"Hi, beautiful!" His usual greeting brought a blush to her cheeks.

"You always say that." He cheered her up and reassured her that she was still young and attractive.

Angelica saw the needle in his hand and wailed.

"*Non*, precious, it won't hurt." The doctor swabbed down Viktor's arm and drew a syringe full of blood. He blinked but didn't make a sound.

Next Octavia picked dubiously at the fluorescent pink adhesive bandage. When he came to Angelica, she decided to stick the proffered sucker in her mouth and turn her head away.

"Now it's your turn." Surprised, Carrie offered her arm as the doctor drew her blood.

"Thanks for taking time for all of them." Carrie watched as Reynaud examined Ion's ears. "When will we hear the results?"

"Hopefully before I leave next week." He pumped a syringe full of something into Ion's thigh. "His ears are still infected. Try to get him outside for fresh air, and keep him as dry as you can."

"I know." Carrie's shoulders sagged. "He just doesn't seem to get any better."

"Carrie." His accent caressed her name like a velvet glove. "He only made it through the winter because of your care. Stop being so hard on yourself." He smiled a crooked grin, and Carrie's mood lightened.

"You're a real shot in the arm," she teased, poking him above the elbow.

"I try." He shrugged elaborately with a mischievous wink. Turning serious, he said, "I'll call you with results next week. Let us pray for good news."

The days passed slowly. Carrie chose to take the call alone. Not that the children would understand, but she didn't want to be distracted. Both elbows planted on Sister Pauline's desk, Carrie held the receiver to her ear. "Carrie Randolph here."

"*Bon jour!* Congratulations! You may tell Mr. Romero that

Viktor is fine. Undersized for his age, understandable in the circumstances, but in good health otherwise."

"The tests were negative?" She wanted to confirm.

"His test, yes."

Oh, no!

"Brace yourself, *mon petite.*"

"It's Ion, isn't it?" Her worst fears were realized.

"Not Ion, although he is very sick."

"Who—?" Carrie couldn't bring herself to finish the question.

"Octavia. She tested positive for HIV."

Tears blinded Carrie. Poor Octavia, so often unhappy, now denied even the slim chance for adoption, and with a short, horrible future awaiting her. Carrie swallowed past the lump in her throat and spoke in a shaky voice. "Thanks for calling me, Doctor."

"I wish I had better news for you. Now a word about another patient—"

"Can anything be done for Angelica?"

"I believe so. I'm working on getting together a surgical team. But I'm talking about you. You have lost too much weight. You cannot care for the children if you don't take care of yourself first. We are concerned about you. Eat right, get plenty of rest—"

"And call the doctor in the morning?" Carrie tried to joke past her heaving throat. "Thanks for your concern. I will try."

They said good-bye, and Carrie continued staring at the phone in stunned silence. *How stupid.* She had hoped all of her children would be spared the killer virus. She wiped her hands on her jeans. How many times had she changed Octavia's diaper? Had she always washed her hands? She could have caught the virus herself!

Terror froze her for a few moments, visions of HIV racing through her veins like dye. Her hands rested on a book left by the phone. She glanced at the title: *Living with Children with AIDS*. Thumbing through the book, she noticed hundreds of practical suggestions. Trust Sister Pauline to find the right way to equip her to help. She must have known.

What a day! One more thread cut in the strings that bound Viktor to Romania. A new grief to bear, the news about Octavia. What had she been reading in the Psalms? "There be many who say, Who will shew us any good? Lord, lift thou up the light of thy countenance upon us." Faith, the evidence of things not seen, was all she could cling to on a day like this. It couldn't get much worse.

Sister Pauline quietly walked into the room. "I have been praying for you and Octavia in the chapel."

"Thank you." Carrie picked up the book. "May I take this to read?"

"Of course." The director settled her body in the hard-back chair. "This may not be the best time to tell you, but I thought you would want to know as soon as possible."

Carrie only half paid attention.

"Your application to adopt one of our children has been denied by the board of directors."

ten

"Your application has been denied." The words echoed around the room, mocking the snapshots of children taped to the walls. They pierced Carrie's heart, draining her of hope.

Why? Oh, Sister Pauline had offered an explanation. She was too young and inexperienced. She had no means of support. Try again in a few years when she had established a home for herself.

It's wrong! Unfair! Suddenly the heavy blankets smothered her, and she twisted in the bed.

I'm good with the children. They know that. I'll find a job. Haven't I proven myself? How can they say no?

She turned on her back and stared at the ceiling. *Maybe the sisters really don't like me. Maybe they think I'm doing a poor job with the children, and they'll be glad to see me go when my time is done.*

Unable to sleep, she flipped back over. *Octavia! Who's going to hold and comfort you when I'm gone?* She buried her face in the pillow, tears drenching the pillowcase.

"Take tomorrow off if you need to," Sister Pauline had advised. *"You've had several hard knocks in a row." No need to set the alarm.*

Viktor. Adrian. Octavia. No adoption. Broken images swirled through Carrie's brain until she fell into an exhausted sleep.

Brilliant sunshine burned through the windows by the time Carrie roused the following morning. She stretched, luxuriating in the well-rested feeling, until the momentary confusion of waking passed.

They rejected my application. She sat bolt upright in bed, propping her elbows on her knees and staring out the window. Tears welled, and she wiped them away angrily. Today she wanted to laugh, to plan, to think. Crying wasn't going to solve anything.

Underlying anger wouldn't dissipate so easily. *Immature? Irresponsible? I'll show them irresponsible,* Carrie thought crossly as she pulled on a worn pair of jeans. Unwanted guilt at deserting the children, even if only for one day, stole from the rest that washed through her muscles and bones.

Resolutely, she pushed it aside. Let the hoity-toity board take care of the children today if they didn't like the job she was doing.

Soon she boarded a bus headed for downtown Bucharest. She avoided the American section where she usually met with Michelle. The bus rolled through the city, reaching a park she had never noticed before.

Carrie disembarked, bought a sandwich from a street vendor, and headed toward the park. Ducks, returning north after winter, followed her, searching the dirt at her feet for bread crumbs. She sat down on a bench overlooking a pond and ate her meal, crumbling the last few bites for the birds. Crushing the waxed paper in her hands, she started to stuff it in her pocket to throw away later.

Why bother? Smashing it into a ball, she tossed it hard and high into the air, watching it come back to earth with a mild splash in the middle of the lake.

I used to be good at this. Carrie picked up a handful of stones and skipped one across the water. Rings spun out from the point of landing. Five stones, one for each child, plopped in the lake, the puddles of waves carrying her hopes until they flattened and disappeared. She watched the circles spread farther and farther, reaching to America in her imagination. Angrily, she threw a handful all at once.

Ducks took flight and flew to the relative safety of the middle of the pond. Behind her children's voices called to one another, feet pounding across the concrete in pursuit of the birds. A couple of preschoolers materialized at Carrie's side. Behind them she could see their mother slowly following, pushing a baby carriage, a toddler clinging to her skirts.

The young boy stood, bread crust in hand, staring after the ducks with longing.

"Don't worry, they'll be back," Carrie told him. She couldn't help herself. She was a sucker for kids.

The boy smiled shyly and held up the bread for her inspection. Squatting on her haunches, she took some crumbs and threw them on the water. His mother pulled alongside and reprimanded him. "Leave the lady alone."

Carrie stood up abruptly. Hadn't she come to the park to escape ever-present children? With a word of apology to the mother, Carrie sat down on the park bench and pulled out the romance novel Michelle had supplied her with at their last meeting.

The story focused on a young woman just out of college who made the mistake of falling in love with her employer, a man struggling to raise twin boys alone. Three chapters into the story, where the heroine made a fool of herself in front of the hero, she slammed the book shut. The fantasy hit too close to the truth of her feelings about Viktor and his father-to-be.

The mother had moved down the banks with the older children, leaving her baby in a stroller about five yards away from Carrie. Talk about irresponsible! The stroller was poised on an embankment, ready to roll into the water. *Maybe I should move it back.* She walked over to check.

Inside the carriage a newborn slept peacefully, wrinkled red face surrounded by soft pink blankets. Of its own will, Carrie's hand sneaked out and stroked the soft cheek. *If this were my child, I'd never let her out of my sight.*

Without thinking about what she was doing, Carrie found

the baby in her arms. Tiny limbs stretched and a smile fled across the tulip mouth. Carrie pushed the blankets back, running her fingers over the thick pelt of dark hair. The baby opened one eye, a brilliant black that suggested her eyes would eventually be a lively brown.

"You're beautiful," Carrie cooed to the infant. "I wish I could take you home with me."

She held the baby in her arms and pushed the stroller to a safer spot further up the bank. *I could just walk away with the baby, and no one would know.* The baby scrunched her face, and Carrie adjusted the bundle in her arms. Forget about red tape and rejected applications. Baby in arms, Carrie sat on the bench.

Tiny fingers curled around Carrie's hand and dragged it in the direction of the pursed mouth. She laughed, and found herself talking in an absurd baby talk, part English, part Romanian, mostly gibberish that was so humorous in others.

"Get away from my baby!" a woman shrieked.

Startled, Carrie loosened her hold on the infant, and she clapped her knees together to prevent the baby from slipping through. The boy darted in front of her and planted his hands on his hips. "That's my sister," he accused.

"I know." Hurriedly Carrie tucked the baby back in the stroller. "She's beautiful."

The mother puffed to a stop in front of Carrie. In a voice as angry as her face was red, she launched a volley of speech so loud, so fast, and so obscene, that it exceeded Carrie's ability in Romanian. The meaning was unmistakable. *Get your dirty hands off my baby. Go back home where you belong before I call the police.*

Carrie stumbled blindly away from the park. What was she thinking? How had she sunk so low that—the word stuck in her throat—kidnapping would even occur to her? She climbed on the first bus that came by, not much caring where it was headed.

The bus passed recognizable landmarks. It was headed downtown by a route that would take them past Radu's church. The blocks rumbled by, barely registering on Carrie's consciousness. As if by instinct, she got out at the church and stumbled into the sanctuary.

She ran to the altar and flung herself down on her knees. Great, choking sobs shook her body. Words formed in her mind but couldn't push past the tears in her throat. *Help. Forgive me.*

Eventually the crying subsided, and Carrie sat back in a pew. The Madonna and child shining as the centerpiece of the Tree of Jesse mocked her. *All I want is to adopt a child. What is so wrong about that?* Tears filled her eyes again. Oh, she knew the answers. God's timing didn't have to match hers. It still might happen—some day. But she was twenty-three and lonely and far from home.

"I am with you always." Jesus' words reassured her. *"You are not alone."*

Even when I've made such a fool of myself?

"Always. Nothing separates you from My love."

Carrie moved closer to the fresco, fingers tracing the branches that linked the heroes of faith. They rested on Sarah—ninety before she had her precious baby Isaac. Rachel watched her sister give birth to son after son while her arms ached to hold a child. But they believed and persevered and in due time they were rewarded.

So if not yet, what should I do now? The theme of waiting repeated itself along the branches of the tree. David caught her attention, crowned king more than a decade after Samuel first anointed him.

Ten years. In ten years, she would be thirty-three years old. She couldn't imagine being over thirty.

What did David do while he was waiting? Watch himself

grow older year by year? Certainly not. She ticked off things he accomplished during that decade. He worked. He prayed. He made friends. He fell in love. He prepared himself.

In other words, he went about life as usual. For her, that meant going back to the home. Back to the children God had called her to help.

And after Romania? Home to look for a job? Fall in love? Unbidden, Steve's face formed in her mind. He exemplified so many things she admired in a man. Handsome, yes, but more than that, compassionate, great with kids, a talented musician to top it all off—and he was Viktor's father.

Viktor. When he left, she would miss him terribly. Again she cried, soft tears that washed away the frustration. God was at work. She would have to trust Him.

And maybe when Steve returned in a few weeks, she could show him a new Carrie—a woman, not just a glorified babysitter.

❧

"Two weeks?" Steve couldn't help it, a hysterical note of despair vibrated in his voice.

"Two weeks." The Romanian attorney Steve had engaged to help with the adoption, stated firmly.

"But—" Steve swallowed his disappointment. Lost revenue from summer teaching jobs, the Victory Singers tour he was missing, the overwhelming desire to claim Viktor as his son, now—none of his reasons for impatience could turn the wheels any faster. "I'll call you on the twenty-second, then."

The lawyer smiled as if he were doing Steve an enormous favor and pumped his hand with a powerful handshake. "Don't worry. Soon you and Viktor will be traveling to America together. Miss Randolph has done a lot of the groundwork."

A two-week delay would at least give him more time to spend with Carrie. The thought surprised him as it occurred on his way back to Radu's apartment. He meant he would have more time to spend with Viktor, didn't he? He remembered Carrie's warm smile and her patient care of the children, and he wasn't sure. She was growing up before his eyes.

Maybe he could convince her to leave the other children behind for a day. A day alone with Viktor and Carrie. He grinned. What a terrific idea!

❧

Five shirts, all chosen for simplicity of care and durability, draped across the bed. Steve had packed light, as usual. Why was he having such a hard time deciding what to wear? He needed something casual that he could run in comfortably; but to be honest with himself, he wanted to look his best. Blue? No, too predictable.

"I'd wear the yellow. It makes your eyes shine." Michelle's voice startled Steve. As usual, she had stopped by Radu and Anika's before starting work for the day.

Lila always said he looked good in yellow. "Yellow it is, then. Thanks." Steve refolded the other shirts and packed them away. He buttoned on the shirt, leaving the top buttonhole open, and reached with one hand for the cuffs.

"Let me help you." Michelle snapped the buttons in place in seconds. "There." Stepping back, she looked him over from head to toe. "You'll do. You're spending the day with Carrie." It was a statement, not a question.

"And Viktor." How did she know? "We thought it might be good for him to spend time with me without the other children around."

"Maybe I'll have better luck another time." Michelle grinned at him impishly. "Have fun."

She waved to someone in another room, signaling that she was almost ready. "And by the way, Carrie adores peanut butter cups if you can find them. The superstore is a good place to try." She left.

Shining eyes? Peanut butter cups? Did Michelle think he was interested in Carrie?

Further consideration of the question was postponed by the arrival of Carrie herself. She wore a bright red T-shirt adorned with smiling teddy bears, as cheerful in appearance as her sunshiny spirit.

At her side, no longer a babe in arms, a bigger, taller Viktor emerged, recorder clutched in his left hand. Steve fought the urge to crush the boy to his chest.

Viktor. Everyone else—Carrie, Pauline, Michelle—faded away as he saw the boy for the first time since Christmas.

The boy looked up at Carrie, who nodded her reassurance. He lifted the instrument to his lips, and notes streamed out, first "Frère Jacques" and then a remarkable rendition of "Victory in Jesus."

No one spoke into the silence. Dropping to his knees, Steve looked Viktor in the eye. "That was beautiful! Thank you for the music!"

Carrie repeated his words in Romanian, but before she finished translating, Steve leaned over and kissed the top of Viktor's head, tears of joy dampening his hair. He squeezed him briefly. "It's good to see you again."

Carrie stared at him, a look of sadness mixed with resignation clear on her face. "You two really connect. I'm glad you found each other." Her expression transformed into a let's-pretend-everything-is-okay-with-the-world look. "The picnic is packed. Let's go."

Steve resisted the urge to probe the obviously false tone of her statement. If she wanted to keep Viktor with her so much that she would deny him a chance for a better life in America—no, that couldn't be. The student who stayed by Lila's side at the hospital, the young woman who postponed her career to work long, lonely hours in an orphanage half a world away from friends and family, might be inclined to be immature, naive even, but she was basically kind and compassionate. Although she was sad about Viktor, something more troubled her.

They picnicked high above the Dimbovita River, where they could hear the dull roar of rushing water and raucous cries of seagulls. Steve suspected that closer to the river the stench of pollution would drive them away.

Carrie fluffed out a quilt and anchored two corners with the picnic basket and her purse. "Ready to play ball?"

"Sure, but I didn't bring anything."

"I did." She grinned. From the depths of her bag she extracted a bright red ball, the kind he'd seen on sale for ninety-nine cents in Denver supermarkets but as out of place here as a snowstorm in Tucson.

She tossed the ball at Steve, who caught it in his chest.

"I have to warn you. I'm not much good at this." He threw the ball on to Viktor.

It landed at his feet. He stared at it, then at Steve, as if uncertain what to do.

Steve gestured with his fingers, pointing at himself. "C'mon, kick it back to me."

With a tentative nudge of his foot, Viktor rolled the ball in Steve's direction. In turn, he angled it toward Carrie. She gave it a booming kick that bounced halfway down the hill.

"Sorry!" Long hair flapped against her back as she sprang down the hillside with the energy of a solar-powered battery. Viktor shifted to the edge of the hill where he could see her better.

"Don't worry, fella, she'll be right back. She's just gone after the ball." As if she heard him, she hoisted the ball over her head. "Got it!"

She chugged back up the incline, face flushed red, mud and grass stains smeared on her teddy bear shirt. Her earlier hesitation had disappeared, replaced by a vibrating *joie de vivre* and complete lack of self-consciousness.

"Let me take that." He reached for the ball.

"Come and get it." She ran an end zone pattern and evaded his hands.

"American football now, is it?" Giving chase, he caught up with her after ten yards, throwing his arms around her in a light tackle. They crashed to the ground and rolled, his arms offering protection to her limbs against the hard ground.

The ball stopped a few feet away as they stared at each other for a breathless moment. Something stirred in Steve that he thought long dead. Carrie's upper lip glistened, and he leaned in—

"Mama! Play ball?"

Viktor materialized at their side, red ball clutched in two hands.

Steve stood up, heat flushing through his face. Unscrewing a water bottle, he dribbled it over his hair and forehead before gulping down half the contents. Slowly the heat subsided.

What was I thinking? I almost kissed her. Steve looked where Carrie knocked the ball around in the grass with Viktor. Seeing her pink cheeks and infectious smile, a vibrant image of young womanhood, stirred him uneasily. *I wish I had.* Desire struck him with the force of a knockout punch.

Something hit his ankle.

"Got you!" Carrie laughed.

He steadied his breathing. If she could pretend nothing had happened, so could he. After all, he wanted to focus on Viktor, didn't he?

An hour passed before they called it quits. None of them had good aim, so Steve found himself chasing errant balls up and down a stretch of grass the length of a football field. An exhausted Viktor managed only a bite or two of sandwich before falling asleep, head resting on Steve's leg.

In contrast, Steve and Carrie ate hungrily, without conversation. While he was packing away the apple core, he noticed a pensive look had returned to her face. A haunting loneliness replaced the earlier ebullient enthusiasm. It reminded him of his own sense of inescapable loss in the months following Lila's death. Something must have happened to the children.

"Something's bothering you today."

She looked at him, startled, like a doe caught in a car's headlight.

"Does the possibility of losing Viktor hurt so much?" He had to ask.

"It's not that." Tears fell down a face scrunched up like a wet washcloth. "At least, not only Viktor. I'm worried about Octavia—I told you she's HIV positive, didn't I? Sister Pauline told me that now someone wants to adopt Jenica. And they turned down my application to adopt any of the children because I'm too young." Talking stopped as tears flowed freely.

Without thought, Steve circled her shuddering shoulders with his arms and pulled her close. If only there was some way to comfort her, to promise her that everything would work out. How well he remembered his own disappointment when his application for foster care was rejected. No wonder she was heartbroken.

The storm of tears subsided, but Carrie stayed snuggled against Steve's chest, hair obscuring all but sad brown eyes that looked at Viktor's sleeping form with a sense of resignation. "I thought it would be so simple."

The protective urge that catapulted Carrie into Steve's arms subsided, replaced by a growing sense of—what? Contentment? Desire? Startled by the thought, Steve separated from her. Dousing a pocket handkerchief with water, he handed it to Carrie.

"Thanks." The water didn't completely erase the streaks of tears that marked her cheeks, but she seemed more at peace.

"Life goes on, you know." Steve spoke into the silence. She looked at him, eyes still wet with tears.

"You're losing children who are special to you. Too many, all at one time. But just like Angelica took Adrian's place, other children will come. In helping them, you'll find your answers."

"I know." She gulped, almost swallowing the words. "But I was hoping for a family. A child. Someone I wouldn't have to leave behind. And they said no." A single tear traveled down the same path, and Steve raised a finger to wipe away the drop.

A longing to shield her from pain, to protect her, coursed through him. He covered her fingers with his own and raised them to his lips before tugging her toward him. His arms circled her slight body, his strength protecting her softness. Lips parted in a breathless smile, she invited his caress. Cheek to cheek, their lips met. Pleasure as keen as a soaring Chopin prelude flowed through him.

eleven

Steve's kiss flamed against Carrie's lips, opening them up like a blast of warmth from a fireplace on a cold day. Of their own volition, her hands moved, pulling his head closer. His breath tasted sweet, like the apples they had eaten. A contented sigh escaped. It had been so long since she embraced a man.

Steve's lips grazed the corner of her mouth. *Correct that.* She had never kissed a man like this. Compared to Steve, her dates in college were children.

His lips moved over her hair, while his prickly chin brushed her forehead. Carrie relished the sense of belonging, of being cherished. Memories flashed across her mind, superimposing images of her and Viktor with Steve until they stood together like one happy family. *I'd like that.*

Steve's hands moved up and down her arms, sending shivers through her body. A soft murmur tickled her ear.

"Lila."

All the warm, cozy feelings vanished, replaced by a cold, hard ball in the pit of her stomach. Life drained out, leaving her stiff in Steve's embrace.

He opened his eyes, smoky brown irises boring into hers. "What's wrong?"

In answer, Carrie bolted out of Steve's arms and stood gawking at him. "You don't know?"

"Oh no." He looked up at her, eyes widening in realization. "I called you Lila, didn't I?"

Not trusting her voice, Carrie nodded.

"You must think I'm an insensitive idiot." He ran his fingers through his hair then stuck them in his pockets.

"If you want the truth—yes." Carrie stared in the direction of the surging river, trying to bring her anger under control. "I want to leave."

"Carrie, I'm sorry." Steve stumbled to his feet and reached out for her. She jerked away from his touch and started throwing things in the picnic basket. Silence lengthened between them like a stretched rubber band.

"You're a special person. With a lot to offer."

"Obviously not." She couldn't help it; she sniffed. "Not when you had Lila." Mad at herself for being so weak, she savagely rolled the quilt into a ball.

"Oh, Carrie." Steve drew a deep breath, like a whale coming up for air. "Some special man will want you." Taking the quilt away from her, he kissed her gently, briefly on the lips. "I envy that man."

In spite of her intentions, Carrie shuddered with delighted recognition. Maybe her fantasy wasn't so impossible after all.

❧

The phone jangled in Radu's apartment. Anika answered.

"For you." She handed the receiver to Steve. "It's Carrie."

Steve hesitated. Why was she calling? Since the picnic, she had seen him only long enough to say hello and good-bye when he picked up Viktor. Their meetings had the strained atmosphere of a divorced father taking his children for the weekend. He didn't know how to apologize, how to make it up to her. *Keep it casual.*

"Hi! What's up?"

"You brought some medical supplies with you?" She asked in a breathless voice, as if fear had erased her anger at him. "Electrolyte solution? Cough syrup?"

Viktor! "Yes. Who's sick?" Worry swamped him.

"They all are. The flu." A wail rose in the background. "That's Octavia. She's miserable."

"I'll be right out." Steve cut off further conversation.

"Thanks." The receiver clicked in his ear.

The baby supplies—diapers, medicine, bottles, formula—felt ominously light in his hands. There was barely enough for one child. But how could he say no to the others in need? Bottom line was, he couldn't. He'd have to trust God to provide.

He found Carrie in Sister Pauline's office talking on the phone. A fussy Jenica squirmed in her lap. The baby's skin looked flushed and dry, obviously fevered. Finishing the conversation, Carrie looked at Steve, concern evident in her eyes.

"That was Dr. Reynaud. He told me the equivalent of take two aspirin, go to bed, drink plenty of fluids, and call me in the morning." She laid a hand against Jenica's forehead and winced. "Their fevers are so high."

"I brought children's pain reliever." Surely they had such basic supplies?

"Great! Maybe that will bring down the fevers."

Hardly a breeze stirred the sultry summer air, and Steve could feel sweat beading on his forehead.

"Thanks for coming." Carrie spoke in a quiet voice. "After the way I've treated you this week, I was afraid you might take Viktor and run. I wouldn't have blamed you if you had."

"It's like I told you. You're important to me." Steve had to try to explain. "What matters to you, matters to me."

She flashed him a weary smile and opened the door to the toddler ward. The usual stench tripled in strength, reeking of vomit and soiled diapers. Almost unable to breath in the sickening miasma, Steve slowly followed Carrie. *Steady,* he told himself, fighting the impulse to run.

"Take care of Jenica," he directed Carrie. "I'll check on the others."

When he passed Sister Marie, she smiled wearily from where she stood trying to change two diapers at the same time.

Viktor. His shirt bore evidence of vomit, and his face was flushed with fever. Still, he was breathing normally, and he summoned a smile for Steve.

Check on the others.

All the children showed signs of illness, but Ion's case was worst. Nearly every inch of his small body was soiled, and he lay motionless, sucking in air in great, rasping breaths. Smoothing back matted hair from his forehead, Steve cradled the boy to his chest and carried him to the bathroom.

Starting cool tap water, he stripped the soiled clothes from Ion and placed him in the tub. Sudsing a washcloth, he wiped away the grime that stuck to the boy's skin. Once the soiled water had washed down the drain, he left Ion under the running water and fished in his bag for the pain reliever.

Weight? Judging by Ion's light frame, he'd guess fifteen to twenty pounds. Somehow he got the medicine in the boy's mouth, but it stayed there, unchewed.

"Like this." Steve made exaggerated motions with his lips, and Ion seemed to understand.

Once again Steve started rubbing a cool washcloth over Ion's body. So little meat covered his bones—not like Sammy's plump fingers squirting water from a water gun. More like—Brandon.

Ion's chest heaved with the effort to breathe. Steve dug in his bag for the cough syrup. Not that it would do much good. This child needed a hospital.

But they didn't save Lila and Brandon. Steve remembered the poorly staffed, poorly equipped hospital in Bucharest. Maybe they wouldn't do Ion any good, either.

Sobs choked his throat. *Viktor. I can't lose you, too. Grieving hurts too much.*

Steve had done what he could for Ion. Now it was time to care for his son.

Somewhere Sister Pauline had resurrected two rocking chairs. Steve and Carrie lived in them for the next two days, rocking sick babies, sleeping, eating a few bites of whatever Cristina brought to them.

Only three bottles of the electrolyte solution remained. Still-damp diapers replaced soiled ones. Fevers continued to rage. They obtained some penicillin for Ion, but nothing slowed down the fluid building in his lungs.

A third night fell. Carrie slept with Ion propped up in her arms, trying to help ease his breathing. Sweat stamped dark curls against her forehead, trailing down her slender neck, a neck meant to be kissed. Not that she would welcome any more of his kisses. *Why did I ever call her Lila?*

Heat swamped him, sapping him of energy. Carrie seemed to handle the heat better than he did. Laying Viktor in his crib, Steve once again tried to open the head-high window. Grime glued the corner shut, and the catch was too high to turn effectively. He had to get some fresh air. A quick look around confirmed that everyone was asleep. Grabbing a bottle of water, he headed outside.

He drew in great gulps of air, the dampness cleansing away the sick stench that clogged his pores. It was no cooler outside; not much anyway. Romania didn't seem to have the same day-to-day variance that he was accustomed to, living in Denver where temperatures swung as much as forty degrees from morning to night. If only it would rain and break the oppressive heat.

Not much chance of that. No clouds marred the sky. Stars blinked in unfamiliar patterns.

The heavens are telling the glory of God. Familiar music pounded the Bible verse through his head. Nothing like a strange sky to remind him of God's infinite sovereignty and his own frailty.

"Oh, Lord! What more can we do?" At best, the children were maintaining, not improving. Ion's condition worsened regardless of their efforts.

Memories of standing by Brandon's bedside and watching him slip inch by inch back into the arms of Jesus surfaced, stronger than ever. *Thank God Viktor's not that sick.* The thought stampeded through Steve's mind, shame and gratitude trailing behind. No more than he could bear—losing one child was enough to last a lifetime.

Carrie appeared at the window, silhouetted by the pale light. Shamed again by his own callousness, he knew she would grieve the death of any one of the children. What if she caught the same bug? The thought squeezed his heart. *Oh, God, keep her well.* Drinking in one last long draught of clean air, one bowlful of twinkling stars, he headed upstairs for the next shift.

❧

A subtle awareness that something was wrong intruded into Carrie's consciousness, stirring her awake. Outside the sky gleamed light pink, dawn of the fourth day since the children had taken sick. A strange quiet reigned in the ward. Something was missing.

Ion lay against her chest like a leach, unmoving. The rattling, rasping sounds that marked his breathing had disappeared. Had the fever finally broken? Heat no longer sizzled through the blankets wrapped around his body. *Oh, no, he can't be—*

Fully awake, Carrie checked him in a panic. His skin was cool, no, cold, to the touch. No breath warmed her fingers. Refusing to believe that he was dead, Carrie unbuttoned his shirt and massaged his cold chest with her fingers. Not a flutter, not a hint of life remained.

Ion. Silent tears rolled down her cheeks. Death had turned his face pale and peaceful. She kissed his forehead and wept for the senseless loss. As an act of faith, a means of comfort, she started singing softly. "It Is Well with My Soul," "Jesus Is All the World to Me," " 'Tis So Sweet to Trust in Jesus"—the familiar hymns came easily to mind, but they had never meant so much.

"O for grace to trust Him more." *Oh, Lord, I do trust You. I just don't understand sometimes.*

She ran her fingers over Ion's features, as if trying to memorize them. Other faces swam before her. Irina, long gone to Ohio. Adrian, thriving at home with his mother and stepfather. Dear, sweet Ion. Now in the arms of his heavenly Father.

Your work with Ion is done. The words slid into her mind. An image of the boy, running and playing in a grassy field, rose in her mind. He moved toward a group of children clustered around a white-robed figure.

Let the children come to me. Ion has come home. I will take care of him.

Comforted at the thought of Ion at carefree ease, yet grieving for her loss, Carrie slipped back into a light sleep, holding Ion's body in her arms. When she next awoke, bright sunlight stabbed through the high window, and Steve was shaking her shoulder.

"Carrie." His voice nearly broke, clearly not knowing how to break the news to her. A single tear fell from his right eye.

"I know. He's dead." The words sounded harsh, grating against the silence. Unbidden, her eyes brimmed over, sending tears trickling down her face. Steve bent over and kissed the tear-stained spot before offering her his handkerchief. How she wanted the comfort of his arms around her.

"Mama?" Octavia pulled up in her crib, signaling the start of another day.

Carrie rubbed the tears away and looked again at Steve. "I'm not sure what to do with—"

He nodded, understanding her unspoken question. "I'll check with Sister Pauline." Tenderly rearranging the blanket around Ion's body, as though he could still sense the cold, Steve took him from Carrie and carried him out the door.

"Mama." Octavia called again. Her work with Ion was done, but four more children would need her full attention today. Giving Octavia a bottle, Carrie headed to her room for a complete change of clothes and real washing up.

Water splashed over her face and arms, purifying her spirits as well as her body. "When sorrows like sea billows roll—it is well with my soul," she hummed to herself. Pouring water in a lukewarm waterfall over her head, she scrubbed her hair once, then a second time. In the end, her body trembled with cold while her heart burned with grief. Half an hour later she joined Steve in Sister Pauline's office.

"Radu will conduct the funeral this afternoon, as a favor to us," Steve told Carrie.

She nodded. *How does he know what to do? Of course, he's been through this before. Knowledge gained at too great a price.*

Late that afternoon, a small group gathered in the home's cemetery. Carrie had hesitated before bringing the children. But they were the only family Ion had, and families grieved together, didn't they? It wasn't as though they had never seen death. They had, all too often, and they needed a chance to say good-bye.

Across the open grave, Steve held onto Viktor as if afraid he would fall in after Ion. Aside from that unnatural hold, his face was a blank mask. He had taken the burden from Carrie's shoulders for the day, doing what had to be done with robot-like efficiency. Like a turtle, he had rolled up his feelings inside a shell of taking care of business. She wished he would stop trying to be strong and cry with her.

Radu said a few words. "Ashes to ashes, dust to dust," sounded just as final in any language. But like Carrie's early morning vision of Ion at play in heaven, Radu reminded them of Jesus' love.

"Jesus loved children. He told us we had to become like a child to enter His kingdom. Even now He has restored Ion to perfect, eternal health. Even now He holds Ion on His lap, caring for him."

Around her, Carrie heard quiet sobbing. Tears traveled

well-worn paths on Sister Pauline's cheeks. Anika's eyelashes glittered with the tears that watered the ground. Only Steve seemed unaffected.

"Does anyone else want to say something?"

Carrie stepped forward. Forcing her trembling limbs to quiet, she bent over and placed Ion's tool set, her Christmas gift to him, on top of the casket.

"Ion loved to take things apart," she said. "I promised him he could fix my car when he grew up." She stopped, sobs catching the words in her throat. Swallowing hard, she continued. "I'd like to sing a song." Hesitantly at first, her voice gained in strength as she started " 'Tis So Sweet to Trust in Jesus." Who else could she turn to?

"Lord, I commend Ion to You." She stepped back from the open grave.

No one spoke for a long minute. Then, with an amen, Radu concluded the service.

Carrie checked the children clustered around her. All of them needed a change. They were so sick. What more could she do? She was already exhausted. *God help us.*

Footsteps pounded the ground behind her. Steve appeared, eyes grim in a sweat-soaked face.

"Pack things for yourself and the children, enough for several days. I have an idea that might help." He strode toward the ward with Viktor.

"Why? What's going on?" She bristled at his commanding tone. *I don't want to move a muscle.*

"He wants to help." Anika joined her. She must have noticed Carrie's confusion. "Give him a chance."

Octavia chose that moment to cry. Carrie swayed, exhaustion catching up with her. "I just can't do it." She wasn't sure if she said the words, or if she only thought them.

Anika took Angelica from Carrie's arms. "Go get your things ready while I take care of the children. We'll meet you in half an hour."

After Sister Pauline gave her approval, Carrie agreed. A short time later, four adults and four children as well as a few pieces of luggage squeezed into Radu's car.

In Bucharest, they drove straight to the heart of the city, passing the hospital en route. The car stopped in front of a hotel where Carrie and Michelle had once ordered mocha lattes in a fit of indulgence. The opulent exterior reminded Carrie of how disheveled and grubby she must look.

Radu waved away the valet while Steve slipped around to her side of the car. "This is it," he announced. "I've reserved a suite."

Reservations?

Before she could frame her questions, a bellhop appeared and led them to their rooms. Cool, almost cold, air brushed her face, fanning her hair. He opened a door to a sitting room as large as many homes.

Carrie stared at Steve, silently demanding an explanation.

"The heat was getting to me." Already the air-conditioning was drying the sweat that slid down his face, leaving salty tracks. "And it wasn't doing the children any good either. I thought cooler temperatures might help us battle their fevers."

Oh. It just might work.

"And Tim is shipping extra supplies over, which should arrive today. So I'm hoping, with pain relievers and nutrition supplements and air-conditioning—" He stopped, looking to her for acceptance.

"It's worth a try," she agreed. "You didn't have to bring us all along. You could have just brought Viktor."

"No, I couldn't." A tired smile crossed his face. "You're his family." Brown eyes peered into hers, asking for understanding, as if he was trying to convey more than his words. "It's the least I could do. You shouldn't try to handle this all by yourself."

Yeah, we make a good team. If only we could be a family. Carrie gulped down the disappointment that rose in her throat and settled the children in their new surroundings.

Whether it was the additional supplies, the cool air, or simply the passage of time, all the children improved. Within three days, the flu-like symptoms passed.

"I think the crisis is over," Steve commented on the morning of the fourth day over room-service breakfast.

"Um-hum." Carrie nodded, mouth full of blueberry muffin. She swallowed. "It's time to go back to the home." She looked around at the luxuriant room. "Although it will be hard to leave fairyland."

Steve leaned back and rubbed his stomach. "It is nice, isn't it?" He paused, as if in the middle of a thought.

Carrie started packing their things into suitcases. The phone rang, and Steve answered it in the other room.

She was folding the last diapers into a bag when he returned.

"Who was it?"

"My lawyer." Steve spoke the words in clipped tones. She turned, startled to see his face turned pale, and sat down next to him on the couch.

"What's happened?"

Absentmindedly Steve pulled Viktor into his lap and ran his hand over the boy's springy curls. "The president has signed the adoption papers. We can leave at any time."

Carrie's mouth formed an O but no sound came out.

In the silence, she could hear the alarm clock ticking. "When?" she asked at last.

"Tomorrow. The lawyer counseled me to leave right away."

Carrie wondered if the loneliness that closed down over her heart showed as clearly in her eyes as it did in his.

He clasped her hands in his own. "It wouldn't have worked, you know. Us, I mean. Not now, anyway. Neither one of us is ready."

She refused to meet his eyes. He put a finger on her chin and forced her to look at him. "You're a wonderful, warm person,

Carrie. You've been a wonderful mother to these children—to Viktor." His voice stretched thin. "And someday you'll have a family to call your own."

But not with you. How silly. But she could no more stop the thought than she could have prevented the children getting sick. She waited for his next words.

He looked at a spot over her shoulder. "Going through this thing with Ion—watching him die, wondering what would happen to Viktor—tore me apart. I'm ready to be a father, I think, although it will kill me if something happens to Viktor, too." He paused and took a deep breath, as if gathering his resolve.

"But I found myself worrying about you, too. Wondering what would happen if you got sick. Remembering how it felt when Lila died."

"So it *is* Lila." How could she compete with memories?

"Yes. No. Partly. I can't face losing someone else that I—love." So saying, he planted a sweet kiss on her forehead. "And you, your work here isn't done. I have to go back to Denver and you—"

"I have to stay here. I know."

For a long, rare moment, Carrie wished she could change her commitment and instead go home with Steve and Viktor. A tingling sensation ran up her arms from the spot where Steve clasped her hands, a reminder of what could be. Then Octavia tugged at her pants leg.

"Mama go?" she asked, bag in hand, ready to return to the orphanage.

Octavia. Jenica. Angelica. And others, not yet known. They were the reasons she must stay, to give them wings to fly to new homes.

Steve brushed her lips with a brief caress. "*Au revoir, Carrie. I'll treasure these days always.*"

twelve

The envelope felt warm in Carrie's hand, as if invisible hands reached across the miles and touched her own. Even before she noticed the Denver postmark, she knew it was from Steve. *He wrote to me!* Fighting the impulse to tear open the envelope, she tucked it in a pocket to savor during the children's afternoon naps. Almost as an afterthought, she wondered, *How is Viktor adjusting?* It was the first letter Steve had written since he had left Romania two months ago.

"Mama?" Mihail, her newest charge, called for her attention. Shaking herself out of her reverie, Carrie lifted him out of the crib—Ion's old bed. Next came Stefan, with cherubic blond curls and pale blue eyes, who had taken Viktor's place.

Gentle autumn light sneaked through the high windows, throwing a leafy pattern on the bare floor. Her spirit soared with thoughts of Steve and Viktor, and she started humming. "Rise and shine, and give God the glory, glory," she sang as she moved between the cribs. *I always know when I'm happy. I can't stop singing.*

A loud crash interrupted her thoughts. Octavia lay on the floor, one foot caught in the crib railings.

All set to scold the child for trying to climb out of the bed, Carrie raced across the floor.

"Mama," Octavia called, a smile shining out of her rheumy eyes.

A smile from cranky Octavia. Exasperation melted away in Carrie's heart, and gently she freed the offending foot. Cleaning the mucus from the girl's eyes, Carrie thought about

Dr. Reynaud's upcoming visit. *Can he do anything to make her more comfortable?*

More important, what could she do? Somehow she had to prepare Octavia for their coming separation. While Carrie herded the children into the bathroom for their daily bath, a partial answer occurred to her: Teach Octavia some self-help skills. Running the bath, brushing her teeth, getting dressed—all things Octavia needed to learn to do for herself.

"Here, Octavia. I want you to help me run the bath. Can you lift the bucket?" The girl struggled with the heavy load; a generous puddle splashed on the floor, but in the end a thin layer of water lined the tub.

"Now another one. Fill it up this high." Pouring water until the tub was halfway full, Octavia added three more helpings of warm water.

"Now turn on the faucet." Carrie showed her how to mix a small amount of cold water with the hot water in the tub to make the water a comfortable temperature. Next she helped her find the laundry.

Proudly carrying in a stack of dry towels, Octavia announced, "I help."

It's a start. Pleased that she had figured out something specific to try with Octavia, Carrie started the day's routine. At lunch, each child seemed to take a minute longer to finish eating, an extra moment to fall asleep at naptime. *Will they never settle down?*

At last, she sat alone in her room and opened Steve's letter:

Dear Carrie,

It doesn't seem possible that it's been two months since we left Romania. Everything considered, Viktor is adjusting well. He misses you terribly. The snapshot he has of you is getting worn around the edges.

Does he miss me, too?

I think of you often and say a little prayer. My time in Romania already seems like a dream. You and Viktor are the only realities that remain. . .

He does! Rubbing the page between her fingers, Carrie stretched out on her bed and read through the rest of the letter, reading and rereading special parts. Viktor's first trip to the doctor for immunizations—Sammy's delight at having a cousin close to his own age to play with—the high school band's adoption of Viktor as their mascot. She succumbed to the temptation to daydream. *What if Steve is still single when I leave Romania? What if Viktor still calls me "Mama"? What if. . .* The pages slipped from her fingers.

Viktor marched at the front of the band, dressed in a tiny blue-and-gold uniform. Beside him, walking backward, strode the drum major, a petite figure with Carrie's face. Her arms waved wildly in time to "Stars and Stripes Forever."

Steve walked alongside, smiling his encouragement and delight. *My two favorite people.* His lips moved. *When will you come to Denver?*

I can't. She tried to explain but couldn't get the words out of her mouth.

Late afternoon rays tickled her face when she returned to consciousness. It took a few minutes to reorient herself to the chilled room. *Steve's half a world away.* She splashed water on her face to chase away the loneliness that washed over her and pulled her mid-back-length hair into a ponytail. Time for the supper detail.

Dr. Reynaud arrived in the morning, bringing with him his usual breeze of enthusiasm and hope. "Good news! I have talked with doctors in Paris. We think Angelica can be helped. They would like to bring her to France for an operation."

"That's terrific! When does she go?" Inside she felt like dancing.

"As soon as it can be arranged. Funds shouldn't be a problem; a hospital board member will pay her airfare and other incidentals and provide lodging for her mother. The doctors are offering their services for free." Like two conspirators, they grinned at each other.

"My other news is not so good." He scowled at the results of the most recent lab tests. "Octavia's HIV has developed into full-blown AIDS."

Although she had always been aware of the possibility, Carrie's heart plummeted at the announcement. You could live with HIV; sooner or later, AIDS meant death. Tears blinded her eyes. "Oh, Octavia."

The doctor's hand squeezed her shoulder. "It is hard to understand why these little ones must suffer." She could hear the tears behind his voice.

"What can I do for her?"

"What you are already doing. Don't be afraid to hold her, love her. Help her live as normal a life as possible." He shuffled through some papers in his briefcase. "Here are precautions you must take. We've discussed them before, but they are doubly important now." Together they reviewed the safety tips.

Oh, Octavia. Who will leave the home first—you or me?

❧

The alarm jangled by Steve's ear. He groaned, turned over, then sat up in bed. Time for early morning marching band practice.

He stumbled to the kitchen and plugged in the coffeepot before heading for the shower. Stinging jets of hot water shook him out of sleepiness. He hadn't expected taking care of a child to require so much energy. All the little tasks added minutes, hours to each day. Still, he wouldn't change a minute of happy exhaustion for the lonely existence of the last few years. While the water needled him awake, he hummed—snatches of band music, melodies he had learned from Viktor. One folk song kept running through his head, reminding him of Carrie and the grave poverty of Romania. *How much I take for granted. Carrie didn't have a hot shower when she got up this morning.*

When he finished dressing, he headed for Viktor's room. The boy was already awake, holding a diaper in his hand as if ashamed that he had soiled himself overnight.

Steve hugged his son good morning and started with the diaper change. *I'll be glad when he is toilet trained. Patience. No one warned me that American pasteurized milk would make Viktor sick.*

"Which one do you want?" Steve held up two choices, a T-shirt with cartoon characters and a western-style button-down shirt. Shyly, Viktor pointed to the T-shirt. "Cat."

"Good choice. I like Sylvester myself." Funny, the thing he had thought would be hardest—the language barrier—was proving to be the easiest. Of course they said children learned languages much easier than adults.

Steve pulled the shirt over Viktor's uplifted arms and handed him a pair of jeans. Precious minutes crawled by while the child sorted out which foot went in which pant leg. As for the button at the waist, his pudgy fingers struggled to push it through the hole.

"Let me help you with that." Steve reached for the waistband.

The boy twisted away. "Viktor do it."

Suppressing a sigh, Steve sneaked a glance at his watch. If Viktor didn't finish soon, they might not have time for breakfast. Again. How did Carrie manage with five children? He could use some tips. Looking at the dial again, he grimaced. Ten minutes passed before they made it to the car, heading for the empty field where the band practiced marching routines.

"Where shall we eat this morning? McDonald's? The donut shop?"

"McDonald's." Viktor always asked for McDonald's.

Carrie would be ashamed of us, eating out every morning. Maybe it isn't so bad after all. A breakfast sandwich with cheese and orange juice provided a meal-in-one—bread, protein, dairy, fruit. *Nah, I'm just kidding myself.*

Except for the early hour, band rehearsal was the highlight of most days. Viktor picked out the melodies on his recorder and happily marched alongside the band, leading with the wrong foot half the time but always in time with the music.

A small group had already congregated at the end of the field. Two girls swooped down on Viktor. He stared at them beneath dark eyelashes.

While the girls entertained Viktor, Steve called aside his drum major. "We finally got the music for 'Rock-n-Roll Number 2.' " The band had begged for the song ever since pro sports had adopted the theme. "And this is what I'm thinking about for our uniforms during the Parade of Lights at Christmas—"

When practice ended, Steve ran Viktor over to day care, the same one Tim and Brenda's children attended. His heart twisted with a sinking sense of dread. *A lot of kids stay with babysitters. Why is it so hard for Viktor?* Oh, he knew the answers—fear of abandonment, fear of the other children. None of them helped when the boy started holding back at the door, burrowing his head into Steve's chest. How much better it would be if he could stay home with a mother.

Steve pulled into the parking lot and steeled himself for the battle ahead. Viktor slumped in his seat, not moving. Circling to the passenger's side of the car, Steve bent through the door and unbuckled the seat belt. In a cheerful voice, he said, "Let's go. Sammy's waiting for you." *They say it's best if he walks in on his own.*

Viktor didn't move. Steve grabbed the diaper bag and again gestured for Viktor to climb down. *Patience.*

"Viktor! You're here!" Sammy's voice rang out in welcome. "C'mon in. There's something I want to show you."

One leg slowly descended to the ground, and Viktor slid out of the car, allowing Sammy to grab his hand and run toward the door. Tempted as always to leave while Viktor was distracted, Steve forced himself to do the right thing—say good-bye. *They say if you disappear, he'll be more worried next time.* "See you tonight, Viktor."

Like an insect's antennae, Viktor's head swiveled, and he barreled in Steve's direction, clutching one leg. "Daddy go." He cried.

"Yes. I have to go teach. But I'll be back later." After hugging the boy, he gently pulled his arms away from his leg and left, shutting the door behind him.

A busy day lay ahead at the high school—orchestra rehearsal, jazz band, music classes for the general student body, some individual instruction. Today he had lunch duty. As he sat in the deafening noise of the cafeteria, one of the other teachers asked, "How is Viktor doing these days?"

Raising his voice to decibels high enough to be heard over the din, Steve answered. "Better. It only took fifteen minutes at the day care this morning."

The teacher, mother of an eighteen-month-old herself, groaned sympathetically. "Don't I know what you mean. Has the soybean milk helped the diarrhea problem?"

Steve nodded. "Much better. Although I'm sure McDonald's doesn't help."

"Naughty boy." She shook a finger at him. "I've got some quick-fixing recipes if you'd like them."

Everyone wants to offer advice when what I really need is a wife. "My sister has already given me a bunch of cookbooks. I just have to get organized."

"Yeah, it takes practice." She frowned at something across the room. "Looks like trouble's brewing."

Two upperclassmen looked ready to pounce on an undersized freshman boy. "I'll take care of it."

After lunch, Steve had a free period. Shutting the door against distractions, he pulled out sheets of music manuscript paper with several pages already penciled in. He wanted to capture the morning's melodies before they disappeared.

At last his rhapsody was taking form. In one burst of inspiration earlier in the fall, he had composed the opening. Like he had once described to Carrie, he tried to catch the glory of sunrise as seen from an airplane. Quiet strings and woodwinds suggested the gentle lightening of the night sky until trumpets blared to announce the arrival of the bright morning sun.

Now he wanted to incorporate some of the Romanian folk songs he had heard Carrie and Viktor sing. His hand poised over the paper, mentally striving to break down the unusual tones and rhythm into the standard musical alphabet of sharps, flats, and quarter notes. Intent on his work, he missed the ringing of the bell until loud conversation outside his door announced the arrival of the afternoon jazz band. He stared at the page with satisfaction. Snatches of melody covered it from top to bottom, a good start.

The day flew by, and soon he was at home. A letter from Carrie waited in the mailbox. "Hey, look, Viktor, Carrie has written us a letter!"

"Viktor see." His pudgy fingers traced the familiar letters of his name. "For me?"

"For both of us." Steve slit open the envelope, and two sheets of paper slipped out. He tucked the one addressed to him in his shirt pocket, where it warmed his heart as if it were on fire. "This one is for you." Settling in the big easy chair, he started to read, "Dear Viktor: I am glad you like your new home. . . . Angelica will have an operation to help her walk. . . . Jenica has gone to America with her new family. . . ." Steve let Viktor study the paper while he read his own letter.

"Dear Steve: I am so glad things are going well with you and Viktor. . . . You were right. Right now, my place is in Romania. There is so much I want to do before I have to leave. . . . Octavia has full-blown AIDS. We knew it was coming, but I ache when I see her suffer so. . . . I am thinking about graduate school, getting a master's degree in counseling children. . . ."

Does she miss me? Carrie's letter seemed restrained, as though she was afraid to express what was on her heart. Carrie, holding back? That didn't seem possible.

Absentmindedly browning a pound of ground beef, Steve read through the letter again. Master's degree? Didn't Denver Seminary offer a counseling program? Maybe he could send Carrie a catalog. The thought of having Carrie close by gave his heart a jump start.

A little later, dinner eaten, a sleepy Viktor snuggled in his arms. "What do you want to read tonight?" Steve asked.

Viktor handed Steve *Millions of Cats*, the story of the one special cat out of millions chosen by an old couple. A favorite from his own childhood, Steve wondered if its appeal lay as much as being the one cat adopted as in the repeating rhymes. Viktor joined him each time the refrain appeared: "Hundreds of cats, thousands of cats, millions and billions and trillions of cats."

One more thing needed to be done before Viktor would go to bed: sing at the piano. As usual, Viktor asked for "Victory in Jesus."

Some evenings Steve could hardly sing for the memories of Singers' trips that clogged his throat. Tonight, however, the familiar words stirred images of his first meeting with Viktor at the orphanage, Carrie dancing as they sang together.

Carrie. Two reasons to write: send a catalog and ask for more folk songs. His mouth twisted in a wry smile. *I'm ignoring the real reason. I miss her.*

As did Viktor. Every night he kissed Carrie's snapshot that was tucked into the corner of a picture frame.

After tucking his son into bed, Steve stared at the photo for a long moment. His fingertip traced the broad smile that lit Carrie's face. It was one of the things he missed most about her. Her lips turned up, inviting his kiss. *Stop wanting the impossible.* He stuffed his hands into his pockets and walked out of the room, shutting the door behind him.

❧

Carrie paced up and down the baggage claim area, waiting for the passengers from the Paris flight.

How much time had she spent at the airport, saying goodbye? Most recently Jenica had flown to the United States with her adoptive parents. And of course she had been there with Steve and Viktor.

Steve and Viktor. Viktor and Steve. Their names echoed through her head like the hooves of an approaching horse that caused the ground to vibrate. With their departure in the summer, a part of her had metamorphosed, growing past the need to cling jealously to each child, yet at the same time aching more than ever for a family of her own—with Steve. It was as if someone had changed the prescription of her glasses and she saw the world with sharper vision.

A group of passengers arrived at the baggage claim.

Shifting her gaze from the shadows of the past, Carrie called the children around her and surged forward with the crowd. All smiles, Mrs. Sorbul was one of the first down the ramp. Angelica rode proudly in her arms, arms clutching a gigantic teddy bear, legs swinging straight in brand-new braces. She broke into a broad grin when she spotted Carrie and the children.

"Carrie!" The childish voice pierced through the noise.

Carrie hurried to her side, hugging her. "Welcome home!" Hospital pale, Angelica still managed to glow with new health and hope. For the next few weeks, the children's home would serve as a rehabilitation center, Carrie providing primary care and exercising the reformed limbs. Dr. Reynaud had sent detailed instructions.

The crowd swept them. "How was Paris?"

"It is beautiful! And the doctors were kind."

"Thank God."

Angelica made remarkable progress in therapy. Triumph came at last on a snowy winter afternoon. *She's on the verge; I just know it.* "Come on, you can do it," she pleaded with the girl.

Angelica stared at her, unmoving, as stubborn as only a toddler could be. *Make me*, her stance declared. She sat down and started crawling away.

"Oh, no, you don't," Carrie muttered to herself. Rummaging through the few toys available, she pulled out the old red ball, a little tarnished by hours of play.

"Tell you what—let's play ball."

Eagerly Angelica crawled toward it.

"But you have to try to walk to get it."

Scowling, Angelica settled back into a sitting position.

What else can I try?

Carrie stirred through the toys again, seeking inspiration. When she turned, Angelica had risen to her feet.

"Mama!" With that joyous cry, as if drawn by a powerful magnet, Angelica moved one foot tentatively, then another.

"You're walking!" Mrs. Sorbul ran across the room. "Oh, my little angel, you're walking. Thank you, God." Mother and daughter embraced, tears and laughter mixing in equal measure.

She wanted her mother, Carrie realized with a start. A surge of resentment flared through her. Watching the absolute joy and pride lighting Angelica's face, the hurt ball inside her heart melted. *This is perfect.*

Angelica moved a few steps in Carrie's direction, showing off. "I can walk!"

"Yes, oh, yes!" Carrie hugged the girl to her. "You were waiting for your mother, that's all."

"I don't know what to say." Mrs. Sorbul could hardly speak for the joy trembling through her voice. "You're an angel, the way you work with the children here. I can never thank you enough for all you've done with my little girl."

"That's what I'm here for." *And I mean it.* Joy coursed like adrenaline through Carrie's veins, leaving her giddy with excitement. *This is what I'm meant to do. Give children wings.* She wanted to howl like a hyena at the inner confirmation.

Hours later, she reopened Steve's letter that contained the Denver Seminary catalog. ". . . thought you might be interested in the counseling program." *Yes!* Pen in hand, she filled in the lines. As she folded the papers to insert them in the envelope, she paused. *Why Denver? Reopen an old wound?* She blinked against the longing to hold Viktor in her arms, to feel Steve's kiss against her lips. *Well, why not Denver? Maybe God knows something I don't.*

thirteen

Carrie tore a page off her calendar. June 1st—only six weeks remained until she left Romania for good.

But where will I go? No answer yet from Denver Seminary.

She cinched a belt around her waist, two notches tighter than when she arrived almost two years ago, and ran a brush through her hair. *Item number one on the agenda when I get home: Get my hair cut.* She peered in the mirror, mentally trying on different hairstyles.

Item number two: Catch up with old friends. So many families had invited her to dinner while she spent two weeks with her parents in Philadelphia, she doubted that she could see them all.

Thinking of friends. *Will Steve and Viktor come to the Victory Singers reunion?* In his last letter, Steve wasn't sure if they would make the trip. Her heart tugged in opposite directions. How she longed to see them both again. For Viktor's sake, maybe it was best if she didn't see him for a while. The sooner he forgot about her and Romania, the easier his adjustment to his new life would be. *But I'll never forget him. Or his father. And what will happen if I go to Denver?*

Carrie checked the mailbox on her way to the toddler ward. Nothing yet.

"Good morning," Sister Marie called, cheerful as ever, as Carrie topped the stairs. "They are all awake, I think."

"Terrific." Bittersweet feelings, an eagerness to squeeze in every possible minute mixed with a distancing to deaden the pain of separation, filled these last days with her charges. In fact, one of her final challenges was how to prepare the precious children, who had come to depend on her, for her departure.

How can I even think about leaving? But I must! Sealing the pain away in a corner of her heart, she pushed the door open.

"Mama!" Even though Zizi had only been at the home since Angelica's departure two months earlier, she already clung to Carrie. Her parents had died in a car accident. Carrie hoped she would be adopted soon.

Unlike Octavia, for whom adoption was impossible. Each day her cry seemed weaker, her limbs thinner, as AIDS took hold. Her diseased body couldn't fight off illness anymore. Another winter cold might kill her. The only remaining child from her original group, she was more precious to Carrie than ever.

Setting the girls on the floor, Carrie collected Stefan and Mihail. "Bath time!" she called, heading for the doors.

She sneaked a look at the clock. Nine o'clock. At least four more hours remained until she could check on the mail again. Octavia confidently mixed hot water with the cold tap water. *Mission accomplished.* In addition to the bath, Carrie had shown her how to brush her hair and teeth and other basic skills appropriate for an almost five-year-old. *But who will take care of you when you are too weak to get out of bed?*

"Trust Me."

I know they're Your children, Lord. Thank You for reminding me. She turned her attention back to the daily routine.

When Carrie returned to her room after lunch, Sister Pauline was waiting. "You received a letter. I believe it's the one you are waiting for."

Carrie grabbed the envelope and stared at it a long moment. Denver Seminary's logo glistened in the upper left-hand corner.

What does it say? She almost feared to open it, in case they said no.

"Remember God is in control," the director encouraged her. "Go ahead and open it."

As usual, she seems to know what I'm thinking. Slipping a

thumbnail under the flap of the envelope, Carrie tore it open.

"Congratulations! You have been accepted to begin work in the counseling program. . .invaluable insight from your work in Romania. . . ."

"Hooray!" Carrie hopped and leaped from sheer joy and relief.

"Praise God," Sister Pauline said quietly. "You have taken another step on the way to the work God created you to do."

Carrie hugged the older woman, mentor, friend, and spiritual counselor all in one. "Thank you." Feeling the brittle shoulder bones beneath her fingers, she could hardly imagine that the elderly woman was ever young or insecure. "I suspect that whenever I wonder what to do, I will ask myself, 'What would Sister Pauline do?' "

The tiny saint chuckled. "Keep your eyes fixed on the Lord," she gently chided. "Now I must return to my work." She closed the door behind her.

She means she must return to prayer. That's her work.

Carrie's feet skipped. *Thank You, Lord!* Nestled against the backdrop of the Rocky Mountains she had never seen, Denver Seminary had emerged her first choice for graduate school. She could continue her grounding in the Bible, in ministry, and in counseling, all at the same time.

And it's close to Steve and Viktor, she reminded herself, not for the first time. She shut the thought out. There were a lot of good reasons for going to Denver. Not many seminaries offered a degree in counseling. The Romeros, father and son, were only an added bonus.

❧

Steve laid down his pencil and slumped in his chair. Fighting for the right melodies and instruments to carry the overwhelming loss of wife and son had proved a difficult catharsis of spirit. *I loved you, Lila. I will always miss you. But I don't think about you all the time anymore.*

Checking the clock, he decided he had time to assemble

Viktor's new swing set before the boy woke up from his nap. He dragged the heavy box outside. While he twisted the pipes together, squinting against the sun, he tried to figure out the instructions. It looked so easy when the salesman did it in the store. He had long ago resigned himself to being quick with his fingers but not with his hands. Grinding his teeth, he tried one more time. There! Half the frame was complete.

The patio door slid open, and Viktor ran across the grass. Strong brown legs pumped beneath red shorts, shorter than when they were purchased in the spring. *My son. Thank You, Lord.*

Only a week before, the courts finalized the adoption. Tim and Brenda would join them for a celebration dinner in the evening.

"Daddy play ball with Viktor?" The boy clutched a foam football in his hands. He reached down and touched the aluminum tubing. "What is it?"

"It will be a swing." Steve looked at the half-assembled materials. *There's always next weekend.* "Come on, let's play some football." Tucking boy and ball under his arm like a football running back, he ran to the fence at the back of the yard. "Touchdown!" Steve shouted, thrusting a giggling Viktor high into the air. He let him down, and they rolled together in the grass, Viktor still clutching the ball. Grass filled Steve's nostrils as Viktor plunked down on his back before jumping off. Memories of another football game intruded, a time when his arms cradled Carrie's slender body. A tremor of remembered desire jolted through him.

Breathless, Steve struggled into a sitting position. Drawing in one gulp of air, he said, "Let's toss the ball for a few minutes."

Rough and tumble play continued for another hour. The sun slanted west when they stopped for the afternoon. Heading inside to prepare for the evening's celebration, Steve flicked on the television for the five o'clock news.

The local sports reporter was giving the teaser. "And how

was the first week of training camp for the Broncos? Stay tuned and find out."

The Broncos' season is starting already? Thinking of the many empty hours he had whiled away in front of the television set during football season, Steve was thankful once again he had Viktor to fill his days with joy.

He checked the clock. 5:15 p.m. Uh oh. Tim and Brenda were due in about an hour. Time to get the barbecue grill going.

An hour later, father and son surveyed the results of their efforts. Viktor had carefully torn lettuce into tiny pieces for the salad while Steve had started up the grill, laid out the steaks, and set the table. The front doorbell rang.

"Uncle Tim!" Steve's heart warmed at the way Viktor reached out to his family.

Sammy and Amanda raced into the room ahead of their parents. Brenda proffered a bouquet of roses. "Congratulations, Daddy! It's finally official," she said, kissing her brother on the cheek.

"Thanks. I have a vase here somewhere." He dug a cut glass vase out of the china cabinet.

"And this is for you." Brenda handed Viktor a package, winking at Steve when Viktor started to open it. Wrapped inside were a faded Broncos hat and a child-sized Victory Singers T-shirt.

"That hat."

"Broncos." Viktor recognized the logo immediately.

"You shouldn't have." Steve said to Brenda. Pulling the cap over Viktor's head, he explained, "Not just any hat. This was your Grandfather Romero's favorite, lucky hat, the one he wore during every game of the Broncos' first Super Bowl season."

"And he wanted his grandson to have it," Brenda said firmly.

Tim leafed through the packet of pictures taken of Steve and Viktor about a month earlier. "They turned out well."

Steve studied the portraits again. How tall, how tanned and healthy Viktor appeared.

"You both look so happy," Brenda said. "Viktor is actually smiling. How did they coax a smile out of him?" She glanced over to where he sat, watching the proceeding as solemn as usual.

"The usual gimmicks." Steve grinned at the memory. "The photographer said Viktor looked a lot like me. When I explained that he was adopted, she couldn't believe it."

Head cocked to one side, Brenda studied their faces. "Viktor does have the same dark curly hair and onyx eyes as the Romeros." She ran a hand over her own head. "But it's more than that. You both have the same shy smile that sneaks up on you like sunrise behind the mountains." She picked up the 11 x 14 print, already in an ornate frame. "Where are you going to hang this one?"

"On the wall of fame, of course." They headed for the hallway. Steve looked down the row of pictures, from high school graduation to wedding to his last tour with the Victory Singers. Carrie's face stared at him from the front row, teeth gleaming in a face framed by short, bouncy hair. *She's here with us in spirit.*

Turning his back on pictures of the past, he tried the frame against the opposite wall. "Over here, I think. New life, new wall." Spoken half in jest, the words sent joy pulsing through him. *This is it. Viktor is my son.* He tugged another frame out of a plain white envelope. "This belongs next to the picture." It was the adoption certificate.

"Viktor Timothy Romero. I'm honored." Tim's voice cracked as he read the name emblazoned in bold print.

"My victorious son in the faith. That's my Viktor." Steve hammered nails into the wall and hung the frames side by side. Gathering Viktor in his arms, they stood staring for a moment longer.

"Viktor." The boy pointed to the letters of his name.

"Viktor Romero." Steve emphasized the surname.

"Daddy." Viktor tucked his head against Steve's chest.

Into the emotionally charged silence that threatened to make all the adults cry, Sammy's voice intruded. "When are we going to eat? I'm hungry!"

Steve blinked away tears and looked at his watch. "The potatoes should be about ready. Time to put the steaks on. Well done for you, Tim, and rare for Brenda. What about the kids?"

Over the meal, conversation turned to the upcoming Victory Singers reunion. "Do you think you'll go this year?" Brenda inquired gently. "A lot of people are anxious to see you again. And they're curious about Viktor."

"And Carrie Randolph has sent her registration," Tim added.

Viktor's head popped up at hearing the name Carrie.

Blood raced through Steve's veins at the mention of her name. Almost a year had passed since he last saw her. Did she want to see him as much as he wanted to see her, or had she changed? *If not me, she'll at least want to see Viktor.*

"That's right, her two-year stint must be just about over," Brenda said. "I wonder what she plans on doing next."

"She's going to graduate school. Maybe Denver Seminary," Steve answered automatically.

"Really? I hadn't heard that." Tim blinked in surprise.

"About the reunion—I haven't decided yet. Viktor doesn't deal well with large groups of strangers."

When Steve tucked Viktor into bed that night, the boy asked, "Mama coming?" He pointed to Carrie's picture that he still kept by his bedside.

"Not here. She's going to the reunion in Texas. Do you want to see her?"

"Yes." No hesitation slowed his answer.

"Then maybe we'll go."

Tossing in bed, Steve turned the questions over and over

in his mind. *Would it be too much for Viktor? Do I want to see Carrie again when we're surrounded by other people? Do I want to drag up Viktor's past?* He started to drift off to sleep before he realized he hadn't thought of Lila all evening. Only Carrie. *Maybe I'll go after all.*

❧

The jet sped down the runway, exhilarating Carrie. *I'm going home!* For a few weeks anyway, before heading to the reunion and points west. "Pennsylvania, here I come!" she sang out.

"Right back where you started from." At her side, Michelle responded. "I've never been to Philadelphia. This should be fun. Birthplace of our country, and all that."

"I suppose you'll want to do all the tourist things." Carrie groaned. "The Liberty Bell and Independence Hall."

"Of course! And I want to check out the Philly fanatic—"

"You and baseball. Don't forget we've been asked to speak at my church," Carrie reminded her friend. "They're anxious to hear about Romania firsthand."

"Yeah." The friends fell silent as they thought about the country they had left behind. Carrie wasn't sure that she could show pictures of the children without crying. *Maybe I should stick to a prepackaged program.*

"Have you heard if Steve Romero is planning on going to the reunion?"

Always the matchmaker. Carrie didn't want to admit that she had been wondering the same thing. "I don't know." She shrugged, trying to act like it didn't matter. "The registration packet should be waiting for me at home. Tim promised a list of people who were attending."

"I hope he does." Michelle dug in her purse for a book. "You two need to see each other again. You belong together, although you don't seem to realize it yet." She started reading.

Remembering the intimacy of their last week together in Romania—the picnic, *the kiss*, the hectic days spent caring for the sick children—brought an unexpected yearning. *But we've both moved past that,* she rationalized. Steve had spent a busy year raising Viktor while she had stayed in Romania. An equally important time lay ahead, earning her master's degree. *But school and romance don't have to be mutually exclusive.* She couldn't keep the thought out.

Ouch! One ear popped. She yawned to lessen the impact of the decreased air pressure in the cabin, and her mouth swung open in sleepiness. As she drifted off to sleep, Steve's and Viktor's voices sang a lullaby in her mind, and their faces danced and merged together. *Maybe he's had time to forget about Lila by now. Fat chance.* Turning her head against the cushion, she fell into a light sleep.

It was only midday in Philadelphia when the plane touched down at the airport. Carrie and Michelle walked slowly through the tunnel, letting families and children rush past them. *How strange to hear English everywhere.*

Trailing behind the other passengers, they halted at the spectacle that greeted them.

Signs proclaiming WELCOME HOME, CARRIE! and HELLO, MICHELLE crammed the baggage claim area. Carrie stopped counting after she saw her parents, grandparents, two aunts, an uncle, and her pastor and his wife waiting with the crowd.

"Carrie!" Her mother was the first to spot them. She ran toward her daughter. In Carrie's mind it took on the slow motion aspect of a commercial then sped up like fast-forward. Her mother reached both arms around her, crushing her close, and kissed her on both cheeks.

They looked into each other's eyes, tears blurring Carrie's vision. "It's good to be home, Mom."

Mrs. Randolph looked Carrie over from head to toe, as if committing the changes that had taken place to memory. Then she turned to welcome Michelle.

The spectators surged forward, engulfing Carrie in the tide

and sweeping them to the baggage carousel.

"You look great."

"How was the trip?"

"Joanie couldn't make it to the airport. She's coming over later." Joanie was Carrie's best friend in high school.

After awhile, Carrie gave up trying to follow all the conversation thrown at her. *It would be easier if everyone spoke Romanian!*

Somewhere close by a phone jingled, and her dad pulled a phone out of his pocket. "Yes, she's right here." He handed the contraption to his daughter. "It's Joanie."

Carrie stared at the instrument and held it gingerly to her ear. "Carrie! Welcome home!" They spoke briefly, making plans for the next day, and said good-bye.

Carrie tried several buttons, but nothing seemed to break the connection. "How do I turn this thing off?"

"Like this." Her dad laughed and showed her how. "I used to scoff at cell phones, but now I wouldn't know how to function without it."

Cell phones? Carrie thought of the one phone in Sister Pauline's office that serviced all four buildings of the orphanage. She shook her head in disbelief.

Soon Carrie and Michelle were ensconced in the familiar family brownstone on Maple Street. By evening, tiredness swamped Carrie—after all, in Romania it was the middle of the night—but she couldn't go to sleep. *Maybe a cup of hot cocoa will do the trick. Like it used to.*

She wandered down to the kitchen, where her mother was putting finishing touches on a cake.

"Mmm, German chocolate, my favorite." Carrie dipped a finger into the coconut pecan frosting.

"Stop that." Her mother batted away her fingers. "Did you have a good nap?"

"Not really." Carrie rummaged through the shelves, not finding what she was looking for. "Where's the cocoa mix?"

"We ran out. You want some?"

"Yeah." Carrie grinned sheepishly. "I thought it might help me sleep. Maybe I'll take a shower instead." *Make that a long, hot shower.*

"Wait a minute." Spreading the frosting to the edges of the cake, Mrs. Randolph handed the bowl and spatula to Carrie. "That's it. Let's run to the convenience store. I need some butter, too."

The convenience store? That's right, they were open twenty-four hours. No need to wait until the market opened in the morning.

Keys dangling from her hand, her mother had slipped her purse strap over her arm. "Ready to go?"

Even at this late hour, cars filled the roads and streetlights brightened every corner, transforming night into day. Walking into the air-conditioned store, Carrie shivered. While her mother picked up a few groceries, she leafed through recent magazines and studied the styles.

Shopping. I have to buy clothes. Planning a wardrobe fit for a princess—the reunion, anyway—occupied her attention until her mother reached the checkout line.

A couple of days passed before Carrie and Michelle made it to the mall. "Everything's so expensive," Carrie complained, holding up a pink dress against her face.

"Uh-huh." Michelle agreed. She pulled out a yellow dress identical in style to the pink one Carrie held. "Try this one. Yellow is Steve's favorite color."

Steve again. "Who cares?"

"Try it on anyhow." Michelle grinned, thrusting it into Carrie's hands as she headed for the dressing rooms.

"Very well." She pulled the dress over her head. *Michelle is right!* The soft color made her dark hair shine, and lacy edges added just the right touch.

"Ta da!" She waltzed out in front of her friend. "I love it!"

"Told you so."

This is fun! Next Carrie searched for a suit. She found one in navy blue with yellow accents and a white blouse with yellow stripes. It made her feel grown-up and pretty at the same time. After a couple of pairs of jeans, a full two sizes smaller than when she left for Romania, and new dress shoes, she had blown most of her shopping budget.

All too soon Carrie and Michelle returned to the airport, a day before Carrie would leave for the reunion. It was time for Michelle to return home.

"You have my address," Michelle said for the hundredth time. "I'll let you know if I decide to move. I get restless if I stay with my parents too long."

"And I'll send you my address as soon as I get settled in Denver."

Michelle reached the ticket agent and received her boarding pass.

"Well, this is it." They hugged tightly in a reluctant farewell; then Michelle quickly walked toward the security checkpoint.

Tears flowed into Carrie's eyes as she said good-bye to her last direct link with Romania. *But soon I'll see Viktor again. And Steve.* In spite of herself, a thrill raced down her spine at the thought.

Two days later, she walked confidently down the hallway to the room where the Singers would practice. Lemon chiffon material swished against her legs, emphasizing her transformation from collegian to young woman. *If only Steve is here to see it.* Through open doors she heard a quiet glissando across piano keys.

Rubbing her sweaty palms on a dry handkerchief, she paused at the doorway. She quickly located the piano. It looked like—

"Mama!" Viktor's voice rang out, and he ran across the floor to hug his beloved Carrie.

fourteen

Steve watched as Viktor hurled himself at Carrie's knees. "Viktor!" Carrie's voice rang out cheerfully. "How are you?"

"I am good!" He answered in English proudly.

"Terrific!" She bent over and hugged him close to her. "It's so good to see you!" Leaning back, she studied him from head to toe. "You've grown." Laughing at herself, she added, "I bet people tell you that all the time."

"Two inches." Viktor confirmed, thrusting two fingers into the air.

About the time Steve wondered if she had noticed him at all, Viktor tugged her in his direction. "See Daddy."

As she walked slowly toward him, lemon folds swishing around graceful legs, he took in the details of her appearance. A new haircut emphasized her high cheekbones; makeup-enhanced eyelashes highlighted velvet brown eyes. She seemed not so much older or taller as more self-assured and mature. Why had he ever thought she looked like Lila?

A broad smile created tiny dimples in her cheeks. "Steve! I wasn't sure if I would see you. Your name wasn't on the registration sheet."

"I know; it was a last-minute decision. Viktor insisted when he heard you were coming." He could feel a wide grin splitting his own face. Impulsively he reached out and hugged her, the way alumni all around them were greeting each other.

"I was glad I got back in time." She clasped his hands between her own and studied him much as she had studied Viktor. Tension built during her silent inspection.

"You're looking well. Being a father must agree with you."

He relaxed. "Couldn't be better."

Silence fell between them. Steve wanted to say, *I've missed you; have you missed me?* but the words stuck in his throat.

"How are you doing, Carrie? Steve, introduce us to your son." Guy came up beside them. Reluctantly Steve dropped her hands and turned his attention to the trumpeter. A skirt swirled against his leg, and Carrie was gone, taking her place in the choir loft.

Returning alumni arrived in waves, everyone eager to meet Viktor. In the first row of the choir, Carrie held court, passing around snapshots and gesturing excitedly. Steve heard occasional snatches. "Viktor. . .Octavia. . ." He tried to catch her eye, but she was too involved in her stories to notice. Vaguely unhappy, he took his place at the piano and helped the instrumentalists warm up. Viktor stood at his side.

"Come play with me," Sammy invited, leaving Steve alone on the piano bench. *How can I feel so alone in a room full of people?* He found himself answering questions automatically.

Tim signaled for Steve to run through their signature number, "Victory in Jesus." After a short warm-up to review songs for the reunion concert, the group dismissed for supper.

When Steve hurried to the dining hall after retrieving Viktor from the nursery, he found Carrie seated at a table, surrounded by several other sopranos, including Lisa and Amy and their families. *Is she avoiding me? Don't be ridiculous.* He sat down next to Tim and Brenda. A hurt feeling gnawed away at his stomach, diminishing his appetite.

Over salads Viktor waved a greeting. Steve searched the room for Carrie. Her eyes fixed on his for a brief second before she abruptly turned away. After that he noticed her studying the two of them throughout the meal. Irritation replaced worry as he became uncomfortable under her scrutiny.

He made sure he went to the dessert table at the same time as Carrie. Catching her by the elbow, he asked, "Is something wrong?" He could have sworn he saw hunger in her eyes, a loneliness akin to the feeling he experienced at the piano.

"No."

"Then why are you avoiding us? I was hoping you would join us for supper—"

"Let's find a place where we can talk privately for a minute." She grabbed a cup of coffee and headed for a corner.

"Viktor called me Mama. Even after all this time." Her voice sounded bleak. "And as much as I wish I was his mother—I'm not. I never will be. And I don't want to confuse him about who is his real parent."

As simple, as generous as that. In spite of the hunger evident in her eyes, the lurking pain that she returned from Romania without a child, she thought of Viktor first. How much she had changed from the young woman who held on to the children as if she would never let them go. He looked at her with new respect.

"I appreciate what you're trying to do." *But I'm selfish; I want time with you myself.* "But Viktor will be heartbroken if you don't spend time with him. Can we talk about it later? After he's gone to bed?"

"I'd like that." She opened her mouth in a smile as dazzling as her dress.

"Daddy?" Viktor stood on his chair, searching the room for Steve. His heart warmed at the wholehearted trust his son placed in him. The awesome responsibility scared him at times.

Tim tapped on his glass.

"It must be time for the slide show. Until later, then," Carrie said gently.

Steve admired her departing back, almost regal in its straightness. When she sat down with a feminine flounce and flash of hair, he shook himself out of his reverie and chose a brownie for Viktor before sitting back down.

❧

Carrie watched Steve make his way back to the dinner table. Viktor hugged him like a drowning man clinging to a life preserver. He fed Steve bits of brownies, laughing at the mess they made.

Joy and envy fought as she studied the family they had formed. Her remaining regrets about Romania centered around Viktor. Losing him felt like losing a part of herself. And she could only have Viktor if she also had—Steve. Double or nothing. Sister Pauline's words stayed with her: "Jesus promised that anyone who gave up father and mother, brother and sister, son or daughter for his sake would be blessed a hundredfold." She was reminded of an old maxim: You can't outgive God.

Casting one last look at the father and son, she turned to greet yet another Singer headed for the dessert table. "Leslie? Is that you?"

They hugged, and Leslie introduced her family—her husband of two years and their three-month-old baby. All around her alumni had multiplied; their original group of forty had grown to close to a hundred. Carrie was one of maybe a dozen still unmarried.

"Find your places, please," Tim directed as he dimmed the lights. "It's time for the slide show."

Eagerly Carrie slipped back into her seat. In addition to pictures from their trip to Romania, everyone had submitted pictures and information about the intervening years.

Slides flew by, chronicling early rehearsals, the airplane trip, Radu and Anika, scenery and concerts. Suddenly, Lila's smiling face filled the screen. The room fell silent.

Steve rose to speak. In a quiet voice that managed to reach into every corner of the room, he began. "You all know that Lila and our baby son, Brandon, died while we were in Romania."

An uncomfortable murmur stirred around the room.

"I wanted to thank all of you for your prayers and your help. I never would have made it through those dark days alone. To honor Lila's memory—we would like to dedicate this year's concert to her."

Tentatively at first, then gaining in strength, spontaneous applause broke out around the room. The tears that flowed down Carrie's cheeks joined a surging tide shed by the group. While she approved of the idea of a memorial concert, she couldn't help wondering, *Is he still in love with her?*

Gradually the applause died down. A new picture appeared on the screen—Steve and Viktor in front of the children's home. "I decided to return to Romania to adopt a child. Many of you have met my son Viktor."

Laughter and applause rippled across the room.

"I don't want to steal anyone's thunder, but I want to thank Carrie Randolph for her part in bringing us together."

Carrie felt her cheeks burning red as people looked in her direction. Although her return to Romania was no secret, she was still embarrassed. Her attention wandered as Steve continued speaking of the joys of fatherhood. How handsome he was, how natural he was in front of an audience. Of course, he dealt with his band class every day. She was more comfortable one-on-one.

He spoke about his students next. "Next to being Viktor's father, teaching is the most important thing I do. I try to make band a place where the students can succeed and learn to work together and feel good about themselves." He ended with a picture of Viktor dressed in a miniature uniform, recorder proudly in hand, posing at the front of the band. Steve looked almost military in his bandleader's uniform, seemingly oblivious to the rabbit ears some students had stuck up behind his head.

Steve had rarely spoken with Carrie about his work. The adoption had filled their conversations. Now she realized that they had more in common than Viktor. They both burned with a desire to help children and young people through difficult times. She resolved to discuss it with him in more depth.

Steve sat down, and Carrie was startled to hear her own voice. "Speaking to me out of a dream just like Paul's Macedonian call, God told me to return to Romania." She had opted for a taped presentation. Besides discomfort with public speaking, she feared she would break down in tears when she talked about the children. There they appeared in front of her: Sister Pauline, Cristina, Sister Marie, Dr. Reynaud, Michelle—the children, all of them. Viktor and Adrian's parents. Ion's empty crib.

"Viktor!" The boy's voice rang out when he recognized his own picture. A couple of people laughed out loud.

I won't cry. But she couldn't help it. The tears came. A chair behind her squeaked as it was dragged across the floor, and Steve leaned forward, offering her a tissue. His own eyes glistened with tears.

"I miss them, too," he said softly. "Every day I thank God for Viktor and pray for the ones left behind." A montage of pictures appeared on the screen. Carrie's voice concluded, "I left Romania with a renewed sense of purpose: God wants me to work with troubled children here in America. To that end, I will start in the counseling program at Denver Seminary in the fall."

"Denver?" Steve's eyes lit up like a Christmas tree. "You didn't tell me—"

"I didn't want to say anything until I was sure. The acceptance letter arrived just before I came home."

Please tell me you're glad I'm coming to Denver. Carrie's unspoken request went unanswered. Viktor climbed into her lap, long legs dangling almost to the floor, and she breathed deeply of his squeaky clean hair. How she had missed him.

Congratulations and well wishes flowed Carrie's way as the

program continued. Graduations, weddings, and babies were punctuated by a few serious notes.

"My father died last year—"

"I sang with the Metropolitan Opera Company last season!"

"We moved to Chicago—"

Soon Viktor fell asleep in Carrie's arms. About nine thirty, Brenda joined them at the table, Amanda asleep in her arms and a yawning Sammy at her side. "You two stay and enjoy yourselves. I'll put Viktor to sleep with the others."

Steve smiled his thanks and roused Viktor. "It's time for bed. Go ahead with Aunt Brenda."

The child blinked, rubbed his eyes, and hugged Carrie tight before he climbed out of her lap. Kissing Steve on the cheek, he said, " 'Night."

About half an hour later, the meeting broke up. Carrie remained in her seat, unwilling for the evening to end.

Several empty coffee cups stood on the table. *No wonder I'm not sleepy, after all that caffeine.* Stacking the cups, she started to get up from her seat.

"Please don't leave."

Surprised, Carrie looked at Steve and remained in the chair. Her heart hammered beneath her ribs.

"Would you like to join me for a late-night stroll? They say there's a beautiful path where the Brazos River flows through downtown." He gazed directly at her, his eyes begging her to say yes.

He smiled, and she was lost. "I'd love to."

Slipping an arm around her shoulder, Steve said, "C'mon, let's go."

Minutes later they descended stone steps outside the hotel to the waiting river. Gentle light glowed from old-fashioned lanterns, and cobblestones lined the walkway. They leaned over the embankment and stared into the river pulsating downstream. Water slapped against the walls in a syncopated rhythm. A flatboat powered past them in the darkness, crowded with shadowy figures and voices laughing in the night.

Another river, another time flowed into Carrie's mind. The Dimbovita. An impromptu game of soccer with three unskilled players. A kiss that brought to the forefront the feelings simmering between Steve and herself.

That was then; this is now. Shaking her head to clear the unwanted memories, Carrie focused on the present, Steve at her side. *We've never been alone before without Viktor.* Giddy with the thought, she couldn't suppress a wide grin.

Steve didn't say much, seemingly content to soak in the atmosphere. Mariachis strolled by. Spotting the couple, they paused and began playing. Trumpets wailed a sad song of love won and lost. Steve tossed coins in the wide sombrero. The musicians smiled their thanks and continued on their way.

❧

"Music. It's the language of the soul." Carrie twirled, her skirts flying in an imitation of a Mexican folk dance. "Have you finished the rhapsody yet?"

"Almost." Steve bit off the words. "I can't seem to end it. Nothing works."

"Mmm. Must be frustrating. But I'm sure you'll figure it out."

They stopped to buy a drink of papaya juice. "It's so different from Romania," Carrie commented.

"Denver, too." Steve sipped his drink. "Have you ever been there?"

"No. I've never been west of the Mississippi before this trip. But I've wanted to visit the Rockies for years." She couldn't say that the main attraction of Denver was the man opposite her and a beloved child.

"Carrie." Steve leaned in toward her and started to speak.

As he neared, Carrie's cheeks warmed. Wanting to cool the rising heat, she gulped the juice. The pulpy liquid choked her, rendering speech impossible. Or was it the energy sizzling between them? Would he kiss her?

Steve pulled back and looked at his watch. "It's late. We should get back." Taking her arm, he steered her toward the hotel, leaving her with the feeling of something left unsaid.

❧

Steve collected Viktor from his sister and made his way to his room next door. He adjusted the child's ever-lengthening body in his arms, and young eyelids fluttered open for a moment. He hugged his father's neck.

Steve tucked blankets around Viktor and bent over to kiss him good night. *Thank you, God, for this child. For my new life.* He thanked God for the miracle that brought them together.

Viktor opened a sleepy eye. "See Mama again?"

Mama. "Yes, we'll see Carrie again in the morning."

"Good." He slipped back into sleep.

Mama. Steve stared down at the sleeping form for a few more minutes. Carrie was, maybe always would be, mother to his precious son; and she was moving to Denver. Their lives continued to intertwine like vines on the same branch, past, present, and future.

Thinking of the future, he wanted to rework the rhapsody's finale. The band had practiced it, ready to premiere the composition at the reunion concert. He wasn't satisfied with the ending; he hadn't found the right note to end the music. *Until now.*

In a flash, he knew what would complete the rhapsody, what was missing in the song that was his experience of Romania. He sank into the chair and stared out the window at the San Antonio landscape. *Is it true?* Looking over at his sleeping son, he reviewed the emotions surging through him. *Yes!* Furiously he began to jot notes on manuscript paper.

Day dawned before he wrote the final notes, and, with a final flourish, he jotted a few words on the first page of the composition. *That's it. Now to get the band to perform it.*

❧

Tim's voice trailed after the choir as they left the stage. "While the Singers prepare for the next part of the program, our band will premiere a new work by our pianist, Mr. Steve Romero. It is entitled, appropriately for this reunion concert, 'Romanian Rhapsody.' "

Carrie stood, rooted to the spot. He had finished it! She had to hear it. Somehow, as French horns and drums rumbled, she could see Lila, and brass proclaimed the grandeur of St. Joseph's. Children played through a lively Romanian folk melody that sang across violin strings. Woodwinds took over, and her eyes flew open. She was right! A simple child's recorder carried the melody briefly, and once again she saw the first meeting between Steve and Viktor.

"Carrie, you have to change." Amy tugged at her elbow. Reluctantly, she moved away from the music that evoked Romania and all that she loved about it.

A haunting oboe melody, full of love and longing, followed her into the dressing room. Passion tingled along her nerve endings. *Oh, Steve.* She shut her eyes against the unwanted pain. Mechanically she exchanged her choir robe for the evening gown and took her place at the end of the line. *I'll have to congratulate him. It's beautiful.*

The concert ended. She couldn't find Steve alone to congratulate him on the premiere. Audience and Singers alike crowded him in an attempt to be the first to praise his work.

Ready to give up until a later time, Carrie started for the dressing room to change into street clothes.

"Carrie! Wait!"

She turned at the sound of the familiar voice, a certain panic emphasizing the words. A smile bubbled to her lips and burst forth as he pushed his way through the crowd. "It was wonderful. It took me back."

"Well, thank you." A look she couldn't interpret passed over his face. "Can we meet later? When things die down?"

"Of course." She squeezed in the words before another group of admirers swept between them.

In the dressing room, Carrie took her time, toning down her makeup since she wouldn't be on stage, slipping into her new navy suit. Checking in the mirror, she nodded her satisfaction. It did look good on her.

Snatches from the rhapsody rang through her head. He had found the elusive musical answer. It evoked mental images of the Romania she had left behind—Lila, Radu and Anika, Sister Pauline, St. Joseph's, the home. The children.

Viktor—and Steve. Playing the recorder. Taking care of sick children. The dreams and kisses they had shared. A pang stabbed her heart. She still dreamed that somehow they could get together and become a family, the three of them. How could she settle for friendship when she wanted a family?

Someone knocked at the door. "Come in."

Tim poked his head into the dressing room. "Steve asked me to tell you that the coast is clear, if you're ready." She could have sworn that he winked at her.

Carrie felt her cheeks flame red, negating the need for the blush she had so carefully applied. "I'll be right out," she called to the closing door. *What's going on?*

With one last glance in the mirror and check of her hair, she left the room and headed for the stage. With auditorium lights dimmed, a gentle glow played across the platform. What looked like a candle cast flickering shadows across the music stand on the piano.

"Carrie." Steve's voice caressed her name, husky tones vibrating from his throat. "Thank you for waiting. I thought they'd never clear out."

"They all wanted to congratulate you." She moved closer, ascending the stairs to the platform. Clearing her throat, she tried to put into words how the music made her feel. "It was moving. Beautiful and sad and happy. Beyond description." She started to cry.

As if from a distance, Steve handed her a handkerchief and started speaking. "I just finished it last night. No matter how hard I tried, I couldn't get it to tie together. For the longest time something was missing, and nothing I put in worked. Not Viktor's songs, not Radu's unshakable faith, nothing."

He took her by the hand and led her toward the piano. Flickering candlelight obscured the sheets of music sitting on the stand.

"Then I found the answer." He scooped the pages in his hand and displayed them to Carrie.

"Romanian Rhapsody." She stared at the page for a moment. What did he want her to see? By Steven Romero. *For Carrie.* A warm tide washed over her, head buzzing from excitement. *Could he mean—?*

"I realized what was missing was you. For my music—my life!—to be complete, I need you."

Removing the music from her and grasping her hands in his own, he leaned forward and kissed the lips that Carrie offered. *I can't believe this is happening.* Delight and puzzlement raced through her mind, dazzling nerve endings in their wake.

"Carrie." Steve's arms had found their way around her shoulders. "I never thought I would love again after Lila died. But you became part of my life—part of Viktor's life—and I couldn't get you out of my mind. Or my heart."

She leaned into his chest, rejoicing in the moment.

He tilted her chin so that he could look into her eyes. "Carrie Randolph. Do you love me? Will you marry me?"

She found her voice. "With all my heart. Yes."

As one their hearts beat in time to the rhapsody that echoed in her ears. His embrace tightened, and his lips claimed hers for another kiss.

A Letter To Our Readers

Dear Readers:

In order that we might better contribute to your reading enjoyment, we would appreciate your taking a few minutes to respond to the following questions. We welcome your comments and read each form and letter we receive. When completed, please return to the following:

Fiction Editor
Heartsong Presents
PO Box 719
Uhrichsville, Ohio 44683

1. Did you enjoy reading *Romanian Rhapsody* by Darlene Franklin?
   - ❑ Very much! I would like to see more books by this author!
   - ❑ Moderately. I would have enjoyed it more if

   ____

   ____

   ____

2. Are you a member of **Heartsong Presents?** ❑ Yes ❑ No
   If no, where did you purchase this book? ______________

   ____

3. How would you rate, on a scale from 1 (poor) to 5 (superior), the cover design? ______________________

4. On a scale from 1 (poor) to 10 (superior), please rate the following elements.

   ____ Heroine ____ Plot
   ____ Hero ____ Inspirational theme
   ____ Setting ____ Secondary characters

5. These characters were special because? ____________________

____

____

6. How has this book inspired your life? ____________________

____

____

7. What settings would you like to see covered in future **Heartson Presents** books? ____________________

____

____

8. What are some inspirational themes you would like to see treated in future books? ____________________

____

____

9. Would you be interested in reading other **Heartsong Presents** titles? ❑ Yes ❑ No

10. Please check your age range:

❑ Under 18 ❑ 18–24
❑ 25–34 ❑ 35–45
❑ 46–55 ❑ Over 55

Name ____

Occupation ______________________________________

Address ____